# Mackarb

R E Barringham

**Also by R E Barringham**

Playing For Real
Two Weeks In Corfu
Stand By Me
What Goes Around Comes Around
Magenta - Campfire Story Book 2
Jackolantern - Campfire Story Book 3


How to Quit Smoking
How to Write an Article in 15 Minutes
Goodbye Writers Block
7 Day eBook Writing and Publishing System
Living the Laptop Lifestyle
Mission Critical For Life
The Monthly Challenge Writing Series
12 Month Writing Challenge
How To Have More Money
Stop Procrastinating

*"Even the bravest heart falters at the edge of the forest after nightfall, for something primal within remembers the ancient predator that lurks in the shadows."*

~ Terry Goodkind, Sword of Truth

# The Campfire

"Oh, come on Harold. You lived right in the middle of the weirdest story ever," said Roger.

Douglas chimed in, "This is the perfect setting to tell it too."

I disagreed with them. Sitting around a campfire by the woods, at night, the three of us all alone, was the worst place to tell them about the horrific events that happened in the woods in the small town of Mackarb where I lived.

It had all happened a couple of years ago and to this day, no one in town, or anywhere, knew the truth about what had happened. Even I didn't know until it was all over. Maybe it was the time to tell them. But regaling the whole story in this dark and lonely setting seemed like the wrong place and time.

I'd been friends with Roger and Douglas for over forty years. I met them when I was travelling. For years I lived a somewhat nomadic lifestyle. I met Roger in Bundaberg and Douglas in Bowen. Both places are hundreds of miles from Mackarb, making it too far for us to meet up often.

We settled on meeting up once a year at a halfway place we called The Meadow. It's a place I stumbled across years ago on my travels.

I'd stopped in a small town in the middle of nowhere, parked the camper van I was living in, and went off on foot to explore my surroundings. I was intrigued by the place because it was completely surrounded by bushland, so I set off to walk amongst the trees.

I found an overgrown track and made my way along it. It seemed like there were hundreds of spiderwebs across the path, and as I walked, I found out that there is no better karate instructor than a spiderweb in the face, but I didn't let it deter me from going deeper and deeper into the bush.

After about thirty minutes I found myself in an open field. It was a huge area and so unexpected after making my way along such a narrow and spider web festooned track that clearly no one had walked before me. The meadow felt like a paradise after being so closed in on the path for so long.

It was so sunny there. The long grass came halfway up my calf and there were different coloured wildflowers dotted around everywhere. If I didn't know it was in the middle of nowhere I would have thought it was a park or a garden.

I explored the meadow by walking the perimeter. On the left and right it was bordered by creeks, on the other two sides it was bordered by dense bushland, the one at the back much denser and darker than the one I'd walked through. In fact, the one at the back was so densely matted with trees, bushes, long grasses, and vines, that it would be almost impossible to walk through it, not to mention the poisonous spiders and snakes that were probably in there.

It was also so dark in there I could barely see a thing and it made me wonder how so much could grow with no sunlight getting through. It must have taken years to get to such denseness.

But the meadow, in contrast, was such a sunny and open place and I loved it.

I was wearing a pair of knee-length shorts and a T-shirt and denim jacket. I took off the jacket to use as a pillow, and I laid down by one of the creeks. I closed my eyes and dozed there for a while, enjoying the warm winter sunshine and the sound of the running water. Before I knew it, an hour had passed.

I sat up and looked around me. The meadow was an amazing, and seemingly untouched place.

I was thirsty. The water in the creek looked tempting. It was crystal clear, and the water gushed happily over rocks and large pebbles. Maybe it was okay to drink and maybe it wasn't. There was only one way to find out and my mouth was dry.

I went to the edge of the water, cupped my hands around some water and drank. It tasted good, different to the tap water I was used to drinking but it wasn't unpleasant. I drank another hands' full of cupped water, then stood up, wiped my hands on my pants, put on my jacket and headed back to the small town where I'd parked my van.

It was more pleasant walking back without having to karate-chop spiderwebs as I went, although some industrious spiders had spun a few strands of silk across the path. As I walked, I decided that the meadow was a place I wanted to return to one day. So, as I came out of the thick woods, I looked around for a sharp stone and made a deep mark low down on the tree on the left of where I'd come out so that I'd be able to find the path again, and hopefully I'd gouged the mark low enough so that no one else would notice it.

When I didn't get ill from drinking the water I figured it would be a great place to camp. I eventually introduced the meadow to Roger and Douglas, and they loved it too and it became our regular, yearly meetup. We meet up in the town, leave our cars, and walk the path through the trees carrying backpacks, food, clothes, beer, and everything else we need for a three-night stay.

And now, here we were again on our annual three-night trip, and the other two wanted to know my side of the story of what happened in the woods in Mackarb.

"Oh, come on guys," I said. "We came here to 'get away from it all' not to re-live horrifying moments of our lives. Let's talk about something cheerful."

"Screw that," said Roger. "You've never talked much about it before, and you were right there. You saw everything."

"I wish I hadn't," I said, gazing at the crackling wood in the fire pit. "I moved to Mackarb because it seemed like a nice, quiet little town, and being in the Sunshine Coast Hinterland, what better spot for warm weather and only a short drive down to the beach.

"And I was lucky to buy the end house on Forrest Lane, right next to the woods, so I figured it would be a quiet little cul-de-sac. And it was. Until two years ago and then it all went to hell."

Shhhhhh...thunk.

The sudden noise came from inside the dense woods. Our heads all snapped around in that direction. It was a quiet sound, only audible because of how quiet it was at our campsite. We continued to stare for a few seconds as though expecting something to appear from between the trees. But no more sound came, and the solid darkness of the woods made it impossible to see anything inside. In fact, if it wasn't for the three-quarter moon and cloudless sky, we wouldn't have been able to see anything around us either.

We camped in winter because it's the dry season in Australia, so we were less likely to get rained on or have cloudy skies, although we had copped a bit of rain on one or two occasions. But this year it was clear skies and no forecast of rain. Perfect for camping.

"It quickly got very macabre in Mackarb," Douglas said.

"You don't have to remind me," I said. "We all got sick of that joke. It's such a beautiful place too. People used to visit Mackarb because of how quaint and close to nature it is. Now they visit for other reasons and my quiet little lane is now a creepy tourist destination."

"Do people still go into the woods?" Asked Douglas

"No. There's always been a barrier across the entrance to keep vehicles out, and pedestrians don't seem to want to cross it either. Nature has taken over again. There used to be a clear track into the woods but now it's completely overgrown with vines and big weeds, and trees are growing where the track used to be. Even locals haven't walked their dogs there since."

The three of us went quiet. We sat in our camp chairs around the fire pit, beers in hand, saying nothing for a few minutes. The mood had become suddenly sombre.

Roger broke the silence. "You've got to tell us now. No one knows the whole story of what happened and no one who lives there wants to talk about it."

"Of course we don't," I said. "Eight kids died. Eight kids that everyone knew and knew their families. It was a terrifying and sad time for us all."

"Harold, I'm sorry," said Roger. "We just want to know the real story instead of the media stories and the local gossip which is all we ever hear. We even saw you on the news quite a few times."

"It was hard to get away from those news cameras, especially when they were right outside my house most of the time, pestering me for interviews."

"You were called the Kenny Rogers of Mackarb," said Douglas.

"Yeah, I heard that," I said, stroking my short, white beard. "I guess he's not a bad looking guy to be compared to. You know, I even had women writing to me. Some of those batty old gals even addressed the envelopes to Kenny Rogers Guy, Forrest Lane, Mackarb. Just that. And those letters got delivered to me."

Roger and Douglas laughed. The three of us hadn't seen each other since before the strange things happened in Mackarb so it was the first time I'd told them anything about it.

Even though we usually met up on our three night camping trip every year, a regular event that we all looked forward to. But I hadn't come with them for the last two years. Coming to terms with what happened in Mackarb was hard and it wasn't something I wanted to talk about. I don't think anyone who lived in Mackarb ever discussed what happened with anyone who didn't live there. Although all the deaths were tragic (and terrifying at the time), it brought all the local people closer together in a strange way.

I'd heard before about people creating strong ties after they share a tragedy like a plane crash, or a hostage situation, and what happened in Mackarb created a strong bond between all the locals. We'd all survived a harrowing experience and no one but us could understand what we went through.

"So, what was really going on up there?" asked Roger. "Did you all know who was doing it? Did the police suspect anyone local?"

I sighed heavily. "There was a lot going on at the time. Not only all the deaths, but the police questioning everyone, forensic units everywhere, TV crews, radio people, and, of course, all us locals trying to make sense of it all, wondering who was doing it and who was going to die next. It was the craziest and scariest time of my life, and to tell you everything that happened would take hours. It's a long story."

"We've got all night," said Douglas.

"Yeah, we've got nothing but time," added Roger.

I hesitated briefly. A stick snapped loudly in the woods beside us, making all three of us jump. We gazed towards the dark trees. No other sound followed.

"Okay," I said. "I'll tell you exactly what happened, but it's going to be a long night. Here goes..."

# My Story

My name is Harold Johnson. I've always like living in Mackarb ever since I moved here years ago when I was younger, and with a population of just over 6,000, it makes for a nice close-knit community.

My wife died after a long illness when we were both in our twenties. We lived in North Queensland where it's hot and humid. I loved it up there. I was born in Brisbane which is about one and a half thousand kilometres south of where we lived. I'd moved up north when I left home as a teenager. I was offered a job up there as a computer programmer with a big firm, so I went.

A couple of years later I met Maggie through a mutual work colleague, and it was love at first sight. We dated for just over a year and then we bought a house and got married. But it soon became apparent that she wasn't well. Her condition steadily deteriorated until the cancer took her during our third year of marriage.

I couldn't speak to anyone about it. My grief was too deep. It felt like life was going on around me, but I was no longer part of it. When Maggie died, a part of me died too. People kept trying to talk to me about her, but I couldn't. I didn't want to talk to anyone about it. All the Bleeding Hearts tried to tell me that the best thing to do was talk about her dying, but what did they know? They didn't know me well enough to tell me what was best for me, and I told them so. They told me

I needed to move on with my life. But I didn't want to move on. I wanted to go back.

A few months after her death I couldn't take their advice or pity any longer. I put the house on the market, sold it in a week, sold just about everything I owned, and when the contract on the house closed and the money came through a month later, I left. I didn't even know where I was going, but I was going.

After Maggie died, I started going to work in the evenings because that was the hardest time of day for me to cope with. The offices were so peaceful at night, and I loved having the whole place to myself (and the cleaners who came in for a short while every night).

Then I stopped going into the office and simply worked from home every evening, and my bosses didn't seem to care. It's amazing what you can get away with when people feel sorry for you. I usually slept until lunch time and used the daylight hours to sort through Maggie's belongings, which was hard, and I cried a lot. Boy did I cry a lot back then, but I had to sort through her things, most of which I gave to the local charity stores.

A few of the people I used to work with would contact me and invite me out for drinks and stuff, but I didn't want to go. Sometimes I'd show up, but only because they were so insistent, and I'd leave after the first drink, telling them that I didn't really feel like socialising. Eventually they stopped asking.

So, when the house was sold and I left town, it wasn't a problem, because I could live anywhere and still do my job. It also occurred to me that I could also live everywhere, so I sold my car and bought a small camper van which was perfect for my new nomadic lifestyle.

I spent the next couple of years driving down the coast, spending a few weeks here and there at camp sites, cooking on my outdoor gas stove, meeting lots of new people, and working in the evenings and into the early hours of the morning when the camp sites quieted down. I also spent my days looking around the local areas, trying to decide if it was somewhere I wanted to permanently put down roots. I also stopped to look around a few places in-between driving from one campsite to another, but nothing jumped out at me and said, "Hey, live here!" So, I kept on moving.

I grew quite attached to my little camper van and loved my travelling lifestyle. Wherever I went, no one knew me, so no one asked about my wife dying, or pitied me, or gave me unwanted advice about how to move on. Each new place I stayed at was a fresh start. Everyone assumed I'd always been single so accepted me as I was. But even so, I knew that I didn't want travelling to be a permanent way to live, but it suited me fine while I looked for somewhere to settle down.

Eventually I stumbled across Mackarb and straight away it shouted to me, "Hey, live here!" So, I did.

At first, I stayed at a nearby campsite and wandered into Mackarb every day and loved everything I saw. I even got to meet a few locals in the pub whenever I stopped there for lunch.

When I came to Forrest Lane with just six houses with huge gardens, I knew it was the place I wanted to live. Looking down the lane, the last house on the left was for sale, a one-storey, 3 bedroomed, wooden house with a huge patio at the back, and a narrow veranda that stretched the whole width of the house at the front. I knew right there and then that the front veranda was the place I would sit the most and I liked that the house was next to the entrance to the woods, which was directly at the bottom of the lane. The entrance is flanked by many trees and tangles of bushes, and there's a metal barrier across the narrow entry track to keep out motor bikes and cars, but it's easy for people to walk around it.

Forrest Lane has no footpaths, so everyone has to walk on the narrow road. My house has a waist-high wooden fence, a gate and a path that leads up to the middle of the veranda, and the house is slightly elevated because the front yard slopes slightly upwards.

As soon as I looked around the house I put in an offer that was accepted and I moved in a month later, by which time I'd met plenty of locals. The first thing I did was furnish the front veranda with a small table and four chairs on the left of the front door, and on the right, a 3-seater metal-framed porch swing with big comfy cushions like a giant sofa, facing out towards the street. The house has now been my home for nearly forty years.

Mackarb is a friendly place. I can walk into town anytime and chat to dozens of people. The main street goes around in a square with a 'village green' in the centre with plenty of picnic benches, bins, and even a small toilet block. The main street was a great place to hang out, until it wasn't. Once the deaths began, all the happy chat ceased. At first, I started to avoid the green because I didn't want to talk about what was happening but the main street around the green has several wooden benches dotted around where locals like to sit and chat to passers-by, making it impossible to avoid people.

Even my house at the end of Forrest Lane was no longer my quiet sanctuary. With only six houses on the lane, all with one-acre gardens, it normally kept all the neighbours apart so I could sit on my front veranda and listen to the sounds of the forest next door.

Usually, the only people who came down the lane were dog walkers going into the woods, who'd wave when they saw me sitting there.

The house opposite mine was empty. No one had lived there for a couple of years. The previous owner, a man named Jed, was a quiet man who usually kept to himself (which was something I really appreciated about him) and he passed away at the grand old age of 96.

It had taken a few days and the strong smell of decomposition (a smell I hadn't known before, and hope I never smell again) before anyone realised he was dead. It was a dog wandering into the unfenced yard and the owner going to retrieve it that alerted to the smell, and he alerted me, so I came to check, and yep, the smell was evil.

Jed's house is an old, one-storey house covered in fibre sheeting. It sits on low, concrete stumps about a foot high. The house is completely square, and it looks like it might have had a narrow veranda like mine spanning the whole front of the house, but at some point it's been enclosed with a low wooden wall at the bottom and a row of tall, narrow windows all along the top, and a wooden door in the middle. Ever since Jed died, his family, meaning his 3 kids, had been arguing over what to do with the house so it sat idle for over two years while they argued.

But then out of the blue something strange happened.

I was sitting on my front veranda late one afternoon, when I saw a man, a stranger, come out of the woods and walk towards Jed's house. He wasn't tall, probably about five foot four, slim built, with a Mediterranean tan, and thick, shiny black hair, parted on the side. He was wearing a pair of beige, drill cotton pants, and a red/blue checked shirt that was neatly tucked into his pants. On his feet he had a pair of black running shoes and white socks. Everything about him was fastidiously neat and tidy. He even had a no-nonsense way of walking as though wherever he was going was important and he needed to go there straight away. He looked like a little guy with no time for nonsense.

Suddenly, he stopped and turned and looked straight at me. It was unnerving the way he did it, as though he sensed me sitting there rather than saw me.

He looked up and down the lane as though he was either looking to see who else was around or watching for traffic, then came to my front gate. "Hello," he said, raising a hand in greeting.

I went to the gate. "Hi. Are you related to Jed?"

"Who?"

"Jed. The house across the road," I said, pointing.

"No," he said, matter-of-factly. "I'm renting the place for a while." I was unsure how to respond because for some reason I didn't believe him. I hadn't seen a 'for rent' sign or any realtors around the place, or anyone else coming to the house for that matter. I hadn't even seen any furniture being delivered there. Surely if he was renting the place he'd have brought at least basic furniture with him, like a bed or a table.

"I had no idea anyone was living there," I said. "I didn't see a removal truck."

"No. I travel light." His speech was crisp and to the point. He put out his hand. "I'm Marvin." I shook his hand which felt unusually cold. "Harold Johnson," I said. "What brings you up here to our little town?"

Marvin looked toward the woods and then back at me. He had an unnerving habit of looking directly into my eyes. I tried to avert my gaze, but I could still feel his eyes staring straight into mine.

"I have a job to do," he said.

I looked at the woods and then back at Marvin, then quickly looked away from his stare. The way he looked directly at my eyes felt like he was looking into my soul. It was as though he was able to look at a part of me that he had no business seeing. "Is your job something to do with the woods?" I asked him.

Marvin looked at the woods again as he spoke. "There have been some wrong doers in there lately. They harm nature and take away her peace. They're savage." He was talking in a strange way, but I was just relieved that he'd stopped staring into my soul.

"You must mean that group of teenagers who've started hanging around in there lately. They're a bunch of local kids and they're loud when they're in there but I don't know what they get up to."

"It's bad," Marvin stated. He turned and stared straight into my eyes again. Geez it was unnerving. "It was nice meeting you, Harold," he said and turned to leave.

"Nice meeting you too, Marvin," I said, but I was talking to the back of his retreating head. I watched him stride purposefully across the road, down the side of Jed's house, and disappear round the back. He was a strange little guy. I struggled with the fact that he'd moved into the empty house across the lane, and I had no idea he was there. I hadn't even seen a light on in there, and I sat on my front veranda almost every evening.

But it didn't matter. I went back and sipped my coffee and stared at the house opposite. There was no sign of life. If I hadn't seen Marvin, I'd still think the house was empty. I'd wait until I saw him again and see if I could get more information out of him. But it was starting to get dark, so I finished my coffee and went inside to have dinner.

That evening I sat on the veranda, relaxing on my sofa swing. I sat there enjoying a cold beer on a warm night, with the slight breeze making it pleasant to sit out. It was quiet that night, as usual, except for the whooping and shouting of the distant voices coming from the woods. It sounded like The Octo Gang were in there again, being as loud and obnoxious as they could.

They were a group of eight teenagers who were a big problem for our little town. They were all about 15 or 16 years old and had bonded with each other years ago and became a gang, who everyone called, The Octo Gang.

They bullied other kids in school and out of school. The police had been involved in a lot of it because often the other kids were physically hurt, including broken arms. Even before they were teenagers, The Octo Gang were always in trouble at school.

Everyone remembered that even in primary school they used to bully other kids. One of the kids they bullied killed himself. Poor little bugger. We all knew it was The Octo Gang who'd driven him to it, but it could never be proven so nothing was done about it.

A few years later, when they became teenagers, they took to breaking into parked cars, even cars that were parked on people's driveways. They also committed burglary whenever they knew someone wasn't home. The teens never admitted it was them, but everyone knew it was.

The thing that got them into the most trouble was when they started interfering with some of the young girls in town. Naturally, the girls' fathers put a stop to that. Some of the teens were actually beaten by the fathers, although the fathers denied it, so were never arrested, which was probably because the police were sick of The Octo Gang too.

They made everyone's lives a misery, and they were all hated for it. Many locals said they wished the teens were dead. And after what happened to them in the woods, people said that the wish from so many must have been so strong that it came true.

In our small town, there used to be a divide between those who had lived here all their lives and "newbies." Even if someone had been here ten years or more then were still regarded as a newbie.

But since the problem with The Octo Gang, there was now a divide between the families of the teens and everyone else. The parents, aunts, uncles, and even grandparents of the boys were harassed and yelled at and told to get their kids into line. I never got involved in any of it, but I sympathised with all the locals who wanted all the trouble to stop.

Many people, especially those with kids that were bullied by The Octo Gang, or had been burgled, or had their cars broken into, started yelling at the teens themselves and many of the local business owners wouldn't let them into their shops anymore which caused further problems. I hated the wave of anger that was sweeping our usually placid little place.

A few weeks before I met Marvin, the teens started hanging out in the woods. It placated all the locals who hated them hanging round the streets at night, but it became a problem to those of us who live in Forrest Lane and to the dog walkers who went in the woods a lot with their pets. They said the woods were a disgrace and that the teens were destroying it and dumping all sorts of litter in there, including smashing glass bottles that some of the dogs had cut their feet on.

I'd even been told that it looked like they'd also tried to set fire to some of the bushes and trees, which is a dangerous thing to do in Australia because once a bushfire gets out of control, it can rage for hundreds of kilometres and destroy thousands of homes and burn up so much of the bush, and it doesn't take much to get it started.

But there was nothing anyone could do to stop the teens hanging out in the woods at night, which was a pity, because we were all sick of them being there and everyone was angry about the damage they were doing. I hadn't been in the woods, so I hadn't seen what they'd done. I preferred to sit on my veranda and listen to the sounds of nature coming from the woods.

But it wasn't nature that I was listening to that night. It was The Octo Gang. I couldn't hear what they were saying or doing because they sounded like they were deep in the woods, but sound always seems to travel further at night, so I knew they were there.

For a while they were laughing and shouting to each other. They didn't sound angry, they were just being loud teenage boys. But then I noticed that their cadence changed. The laughing stopped and they were calling someone's name over and over again. I could hear different voices shouting "It's not funny! Where are you? What the hell are you doing? Get back now!" And other assorted commands interspersed with plenty of swearing.

At first it all sounded angry, but then it changed to panic. It sounded like one of them was missing and the others were annoyed, then afraid. They were screaming, "Tyler, you bastard! It's not funny." I knew who they were shouting for. Tyler Moore. I heard them screaming his name over and over again. Tyler must have still been in there with them because I hadn't seen him come out, but it's pretty dark near the woods so I could have missed him if he was hiding. And if he was hiding, what was he hiding from? Were the other kids bullying him, so he'd taken off? Or had he just disappeared?

The lane is dark at night because there is only one streetlight, and not at my end. The darkness means I can sit on my veranda and not be seen, but it also means I can't see much on nights such as that one when there was only a slither of moon in the sky which cast no light.

As I was sitting there listening to the shouting, a sudden glow of soft light caught my eye. It was coming through the row of narrow windows at the front of Marvin's house. The light was only dim, and as I watched, it began to pulse like an eerie heartbeat. The light was so soft that if the lane wasn't so dark I wouldn't have noticed it.

Every window at the front of the house glowed with the soft pulsing light. I wondered what Marvin could be doing in there to illuminate every window at the same time and make the lights pulse. All the windows had a thin blind on the inside and they were all permanently down, so I couldn't see inside.

All at once, the shouting stopped. The sudden silence was eerie. I looked towards the woods, hopelessly squinting into the dark, trying to see the slightest hint of what was going on.

Then the distant screams began. First one, then another, then another. The screams were so high-pitched that at first I thought it was young girls screaming, but logic told me it had to be the boys in the woods. It rose to an ear-splitting crescendo.

The screams quickly subsided to loud sobbing and arguing, but I was unable to understand a word of it. Then I saw him. Someone was staggering out of the forest. I didn't know who it was because they had white hair and I'd never seen anyone around here with hair like that. It looked like a man who was tall and gangly like a teenager, but none of The Octo Gang had hair like that.

The lights in Marvin's house stopped pulsing but remained softly illuminated, which was the only way I could see the road in the darkness.

The person was walking slowly, dragging and shuffling his feet, staring straight ahead. He stopped and turned his head to look at Marvin's house. That's when I noticed him. Marvin was standing in the dark at the side of the house, staring at the person, who suddenly let out a long curdling scream, so loud I juggled the bottle of beer in my hand and almost dropped it. Just as I retained the grip on my bottle, the screaming stopped abruptly. I looked up. The white-haired person was laid in the middle of the road, right where he'd been standing, and Marvin was gone.

The soft lights in the windows went out.

I sat there shaking, terrified, wondering what the hell had just happened. My hands were trembling. I got up and put my beer bottle on the table, with a shaky clatter of glass on wood.

I heard voices. The neighbours in the lane were coming out. They ran to the person in the road. I heard someone say, "Call an ambulance!"

One of my neighbours shouted to me, "Harold, what the hell happened?"

I got up and walked out to join them. "I have no idea," I said.

The person in the road was clearly a teenage boy but not one I recognised, not with that stark white hair. There was no sign of Marvin and no lights in his house. What the hell had he done to this kid? I didn't know what to do so I just stood there waiting to see what would happen next. It turned out the white-haired boy laying in the road was Tyler Moore. Something had scared him so badly that his hair had turned white.

Soon an ambulance and the police arrived, their headlights and flashing red and blue lights illuminated the whole street. The Octo Gang emerged from the woods. They were crying. The unconscious boy was whisked away in the ambulance, while more and more police arrived and questioned everyone and eventually drove all the distressed youths away in police cars.

I stood amongst it all not knowing what to do. All the neighbours were gathered around me all talking and speculating as to what had gone on. I didn't say much because I didn't feel like talking to anyone. Eventually I wandered back to finish my beer, which, by that time, was warm.

I went to the edge of the veranda, emptied the warm beer out onto the lawn, and took the empty bottle inside. The recycle bin is out back next to the patio so I went out and put the empty bottle in there straight away. I usually leave the empty bottles on the kitchen countertop till morning, but I wanted to get rid of that one in case it was somehow tainted by what had happened, or maybe because it reminded me of what had just happened.

I got a cold beer from the fridge, put it in a stubbie holder, twisted off the top, and went back outside. This time the beer wasn't shaking in my hands.

I was sitting silently on my sofa swing when a policeman came to my veranda and asked me if I'd seen anything. I lied and said I hadn't. Who'd have believed me anyway if I told the truth about Marvin? The whole situation seemed so unreal, like something you see on the news but think it will never happen to you. I saw a policeman knock on Marvin's door but no one answered, and I heard one of my neighbours tell him that no one lived there.

The police and other important looking people were out in the lane and in the woods all night. I'd never known my quiet little street so busy and noisy, with lights everywhere.

I didn't get much sleep that night, and not because of all the noise in the lane. The whole incident kept going round and round in my head, especially the part about Marvin.

What did he have to do with what happened, and what exactly had he done?

Hopefully I'd find out.

# Macabre

The next morning, I woke up to the sound of all the mayhem still going on in the lane. Last night it was all police and forensic people out there, now it was news crews too, many of whom looked like they'd been camped out there all night. I didn't usually see this many people as this in town and now there were many more, all in my not-so-peaceful lane.

After I showered and dressed, I sat and watched the local news while I had breakfast to see what was going on. It seemed strange to have to watch TV to find out what was going on outside my own house. The news report said that the white-haired boy was Tyler Moore, and he'd died in hospital and had not said what had happened to him. Apparently, he only regained consciousness for a few minutes and when he did, he only talked gibberish.

I saw his parents being interviewed leaving the hospital. I recognised them, Teresa and David Moore. Teresa looked like she'd been crying all night. David looked upset and angry.

A female reporter shoved a microphone in their faces and said, "Do you know what happened to your son?"

David looked like he wanted to say a lot but said little. "We're not sure what happened. But it wasn't a natural death. Someone did this and now we've lost our son." Teresa burst into tears beside him. David put his arm around her shoulders and said to the reporter, "Excuse me," and brushed past the media, guiding Teresa as he went.

I felt bad for them, but at the same time their son wasn't completely blameless. He and his friends had been causing so much trouble lately that it wouldn't be surprising if someone had taken revenge on him.

But still, what had happened to him was shocking and I wanted to know what Marvin had to do with it. He was somehow involved even if he hadn't touched the kid. I just knew it.

The boy had come out of the woods alone and Marvin hadn't even been in there. I knew this because I'd seen him at the side of his house. But he had been in the woods just before The Octo Gang arrived. I couldn't see a link between those two events. But maybe... maybe Marvin had set a trap. For a split second that idea seemed like a stroke of genius. But what sort of trap makes someone's hair turn white and scream and collapse in the street?

I shook my head. I knew something was going on, but I just didn't know what.

My attention was drawn back to the news. They were showing footage of the police and forensic people in the lane. On the TV screen it was still dark outside and one of the policemen was being interviewed right outside my house. "At this stage we have no idea what has happened. The other boys who were in the woods with the victim said that he disappeared from the group, and they heard some strange noises. But we really have no idea at this time what happened to him or what he saw."

"Will you be questioning the other boys?" the reporter asked him.

"It will be part of our ongoing investigation. We'll be able to get a better look in the woods when it's daylight and we're hoping that it will reveal what actually happened."

The reporter, a blonde female, turned to the camera and said, "So the police are unsure at this stage exactly what took place here last night. There have been plenty of previous reports of this group of teenagers causing trouble for locals here for some time. Let's just hope it wasn't an act of revenge. Now back to the studio."

The news presenters in the studio were instantly back on. The text graphic at the bottom of the screen said in big bold letters, 'Macabre Happenings In Mackarb.'

'Oh no,' I muttered to myself. Why did they have to put that? Now everyone was going to say it, and no one would ever forget the name of our town, which would probably encourage hordes of morbid rubberneckers to come here and see where it happened. Macabre Mackarb, so good they named it twice.

I went to the kitchen and washed and dried the breakfast dishes. When I finished, I wanted to go outside, to wander into town, but I'd have to pass the barrage of reporters and police to do so. I decided a better plan would be to take a cup of coffee out onto the front veranda for a while and watch what was going on from a distance.

In theory it was a good plan, but in practice it didn't work at all. As soon as I sat down at the table, one of the reporters saw me, opened my gate, and walked straight up to the veranda with a cameraman in tow. It was the same young, blonde woman I'd just seen on TV. She looked to be in her late thirties, or early forties. She was slim and attractive and wearing a neat, checked, matching skirt and jacket. Her hair was pulled back into a tidy bun at the nape of her neck, what the French would call a chignon. She presented as very professional. There was a small, stocky man with her carrying a large TV camera. He'd followed close behind her as she strode up my path, then stood silently and dutifully beside her, like a dog waiting for its owner's next command.

"Hi, my name's Susan Jackson," she greeted me. "Can I interview you for our news program? It won't take long."

I was taken aback by the young woman's brazenness of walking on to my property and coming straight up to me. "Wouldn't be much use," I told her. "I didn't see anything that went on last night."

"Nothing? You live so close. Did you hear anything at all?" It was clear that she didn't believe me.

"Only all the sirens and people shouting, and news reporters trying to interview reluctant locals."

She gave a brief perfunctory smile at my attempt at humour, then said, "Can I ask your name?" This woman wasn't going to go away quietly.

"Harold Johnson."

She took out a notebook and wrote down what I assumed must be my name. "Look Harold, I just want to do a quick interview with you, even if you say you didn't hear or see anything that's okay. It's just that our viewers like to see us interacting with the locals."

I nodded. She smiled at me then turned to her camera man and said, "Roll." She then turned back to me as the man put the camera up to his shoulder. "So, when was the first time you heard or saw anything last night?"

I felt instantly nervous, and wished I'd had a couple minutes to mentally prepare myself. But I hadn't, so I just told her what I'd seen. "I was sitting here on my veranda when a young man came out of the bush. It was pretty dark out here, which it is every night, and he screamed and collapsed in the street."

"What time was that?"

"Oh, I don't know. Probably around 8 o'clock."

"Did the young man say anything?"

"No, he just screamed."

"What was he screaming at?"

"I honestly have no idea. As I said, it was dark out in the lane." I hoped my guilt wasn't showing as I spoke. I didn't want to mention seeing Marvin, but I've never been a good liar, and even not mentioning something I knew, felt like a lie.

"How long have you lived in Mackarb?"

"I've lived here most of my adult life."

"Has anything like this ever happened here before?"

I felt that it was a stupid question. "I doubt anything like this has ever happened anywhere before." I wanted to tell her to go away, but I didn't want to say it in case they showed it on TV. I was just about to get up and go back inside to get away from her, when I heard a man's voice.

"Excuse me, you'll have to leave." All three of us turned to see two detectives coming up the path. They were both wearing suits. One was older than the other. The younger man was carrying a leather-look folder that was zipped shut on three sides. I guessed it probably contained an A4 notebook and pen. "Now!" insisted the older man, talking directly to the reporter and her camera man. The young reporter turned to me and said, "Thanks Harold," before she and her cameraman quickly left.

One of the detectives said, "I hope you didn't tell her anything. This is a murder investigation so you can't speak to the press."

"Is there a law that says that?" I asked, believing that the police had no right to tell me who I could and couldn't speak to. "There is if you're a witness in a murder investigation."

"Am I a witness?"

"That's what we're here to find out. Do you mind if we sit down?"

"Be my guest," I said indicating the other three chairs around the table. The two men sat down.

Of the men, one looked to be in his 30s and the other in his 50s. They both wore dark suits and pale-coloured shirts, with no ties, probably because it was warm and sunny. The older one spoke first. "I'm Senior Detective John Simpson and this is my colleague, Detective Peter Norman." The younger detective nodded and opened the zip on the folder which did indeed contain an A4 notebook and pen, along with a few business cards and other pieces of paper tucked into all the different compartments in the folder. "Can I have your name?"

"I know it sounds paranoid, but can I see your IDs first?"

The two men obligingly took out their ID cards and held them up for me to see. "Thanks." As they tucked them back into their pockets I said, "I'm Harold Johnson." The younger detective wrote that in his notebook.

The older detective asked me, "Did you say anything to the reporter?"

"Like what?"

"Like told her about anything that happened here last night."

"I only said what I saw which is nothing more than what I saw on the news this morning."

"Good. At this stage in the investigation, we'd prefer if you didn't speak to the media. Can you tell me exactly what you did see last night?"

The younger detective was busy writing in his notebook. I wondered what he was writing because I hadn't yet said anything worth writing down. "I didn't see much at all."

"Where were you when the young man came out of the woods?"

"I was sitting right here."

"So, you saw what happened to him?"

"Nothing happened to him out here. He staggered out into the street like he was drunk and then he stopped, screamed, and fell down."

"Why did he scream?"

I suddenly felt guilty again. I had to tell them I saw nothing which wasn't true. "I have no idea. It was dark as it usually is in the lane at night so I could only just see the young guy. I didn't see anything else. He just screamed and fell."

"Where was he when he screamed?"

I felt exasperated at such a stupid question. "Right where he fell. I told you. He staggered out, stopped, screamed, fell. That's it. All the neighbours came running out to see what had happened and then the police and all the paramedics turned up. End of story."

"So why didn't you go out to see what had happened?"

"I was already out." I felt frustrated with their pointless questions. "I was sitting here and saw what happened. Then when all the neighbours came out, I went down there too, but there was nothing I could do."

They sat and asked a few more pointless questions about what I saw or heard before that, but I had nothing to tell them that was helpful. After nearly 30 minutes they stopped asking me questions. The younger one zipped up his folder, and they left.

I went inside to put my cup in the sink. All their questions kept going round and round in my head. I'd had the feeling that they thought I was lying and that I'd seen more than I was saying, which was true, but even if I told them about Marvin, it wouldn't have made any difference. The kid with white hair had screamed and collapsed. Marvin hadn't touched him or even been near him. But there was the strange, soft glow from the windows, but nobody would believe me about that so no point mentioning it. It would just make me sound crazy.

Or what if Marvin didn't actually have anything to do with it at all? Would I really want to send the police to question an innocent person? But if he didn't do it, then who did? There was no one that I could think of who hated those kids so much they wanted to kill them. Was it really possible that someone I knew was capable of murder? Could it be Marvin because he was new in town and he arrived just before the murder happened, right next to his house. Surely not.

I decided to go into town to see what the locals were saying. But first I had to get through the throng of police and reporters in the lane. Sigh!

And it was bad out there. As soon as I stepped outside my gate, two young police constables came and escorted me to the top of the lane, keeping the reporters away from me as we went.

I knew right there and then that Forrest Lane would never be the same peaceful place ever again.

Tyler Moore's death had changed things forever.

# Fear

As I expected, the town centre was full of locals all buzzing with the news of what had happened.

The green was completely full of people. I don't think I've ever seen as many people gathered there. They were all in small groups, busy debating about what was going on. Even on the streets surrounding the green, many people were sat on the benches busy discussing the happenings with others standing around them.

I saw a group on the green that I deemed to be the best for correct information. They were less gossipy than others and preferred facts to supposition. There was also a woman with them who I'd never seen before. She looked to be in her late fifties, a few years younger than me, and good looking, and she piqued my interest. She was slim with long, wavy brown hair, and was wearing a long flowing skirt and a loose cotton blouse, and she was beautiful. I was intrigued. I went over to the group. One of them, Stephen, saw me coming and waved, which made the others all look around, even the unknown woman.

"Thank goodness you're here," Stephen said. "You must know better than most what happened last night, with you being right on the scene so to speak."

I put my hands up in mock protest. "Oh, don't rely on me. I didn't see anything happen. Whatever went on, went on in the woods so apart from those boys who were in there, no one else knows." The new woman was watching me intently. "I saw you on the news a few minutes ago," she said smiling. I couldn't get over how attractive she was.

"Already? Damn they're fast," I replied. For some reason she made me nervous. Not in a creepy way, but in a way that made me feel shy. I hadn't felt shy in front of a female since I was a teenager, so I felt silly.

"Yeah," said Stephen I saw it too. So did the entire population. They're already talking about you on social media. They're calling you The Kenny Rogers of Mackarb."

I knew social media was quick with gossip, but I couldn't believe that something that I said to a reporter less than an hour ago had already been on the news and was already online gossip. "Kenny Rogers? Well, apart from we both have grey hair and a grey beard I don't think we look anything alike. But he's a good looking bloke so I'll take it."

Everyone laughed, including the new woman. I was dying to find out who she was, so I asked her, "Are you new in town or just passing through?"

Stephen laughed loudly before she could answer and said, "Damn you really don't know anything do you? This is Isabel. She lives on your street." He laughed again and so did everyone else.

The new woman looked embarrassed. "I moved into the top corner house a couple of weeks ago. I believe it was owned by a couple who only used it as their weekend getaway. They live in the city and got caught up so much with their work and social life there that they decided to sell what they called their 'country cottage.' They wanted rid of it fast, so I got a bargain."

I was surprised that I didn't know she lived there. I knew about the out-of-town couple vacationing there and I knew it had been up for sale, but I had no idea it had sold or that anyone else was living there. The house was at the top of the lane on the same side as mine, which meant that Isabel was my next-but-one neighbour.

I was somewhat stunned that I hadn't seen her. There was no way I'd forget seeing her. I felt foolish for not knowing she was my neighbour in such a small lane. "I must be unobservant. I didn't know anybody lived there now. Did you move far?"

"No," she said. I lived in one of the Brisbane suburbs. It was close enough that I could walk to work in the city, and it was busy with traffic. I always wanted to retire early and buy a place in the country and couldn't believe my luck when this one came up straight away. And everyone's been so welcoming."

I'll bet they have, I thought to myself. I could see the other older single guys all giving her quick, admiring, glances.

"Well, I'll welcome you too. My name's Harold. My house is two doors from yours. It's the one at the end of the street next to the woods."

"Oh," she said. "I came out last night when I heard someone scream. I was with the crowd waiting for the ambulance. It must have been you sitting on the veranda and then you came down and stood with everyone else."

I was once again stunned that I hadn't noticed her. "I remember all the neighbours being out in the street but for whatever reason I didn't see you. Maybe because it was so dark."

"Yeah, maybe," she said. "Plus, I was standing talking to my next door neighbour the whole time and we were facing away from everyone for the most part, then you walked away and went back to your veranda. I could just about see you sitting there in the dark.”

Once she mentioned it, I did have a vague recollection of a glimpse of someone I couldn't recognise. “I think I do remember someone talking to Sharon, but you were both a few metres away from me and once the police and ambulance arrived it got somewhat hectic which is when I wanted to get the heck out of there.”

I wanted to continue talking to her, but I realised everyone else was talking to each other and I was missing what was being said.

The conversation was going like this:

“So has anyone seen David and Theresa?”

“I doubt they'll be hanging around in town. They won't want to speak to anyone after what happened to Tyler.”

“You know, until now, I was so sick and tired of The Octo Gang and was wishing all sorts of bad things on them. I mean we all were. But who the hell would do something like that to them?”

“Like what? We don't even know what happened.”

“Well, something must have happened. Something so bad that his hair turned white, and he literally dropped dead.”

“He didn't die straight away.”

“Oh geez, don't split hairs - no pun intended. You know what I meant. His hair turned white and then he died. In that order.”

“What do you think the others did to him?”

“What if it wasn't them that did it?”

“Who else could have?”

“Whoever else was in the woods that night.”

"It's so dark in there. How would they even be able to see anything in there anyway, let alone see someone else who was lurking around them."

"If it was someone else, then who? One of us? Someone we know? Who would hate those kids that much they would want to scare one of them to death?"

"Oh, come on, we all hate them. Not one person in this whole town has anything good to say about them."

"That doesn't mean someone turned into a murderer."

"Maybe they already were. They just needed a reason to kill."

"Oh, come one. That sounds like something out of a bad movie."

"Well, somebody did it. It was either one of us or a stranger in town. And why would a stranger hate those kids?"

"Maybe it was just coincidence. Maybe they weren't the only ones to go into the woods at night, and that's where the murderer was hiding and waiting."

"Waiting for who? Why would a murderer think that a potential victim would just walk into the woods at night?"

As the group stood there speculating about what had happened and who'd done it, others started to wander over to join the conversation and some from our group wandered over to other groups as well.

I decided I'd heard enough. No one knew what had happened and listening to all their guesses was just a waste of time. I left the group. Isabel was the only one who noticed me leave, and we smiled briefly at each other. Damn. I would have liked to talk to her more.

I went to the local grocery store to get a few things then went home. Once again, when I got to the lane, I had to have a police escort to get to my house.

When I got home, I put the local channel on the TV so that I could hear the local news updates. All of them were about Mackarb. I kept seeing myself being interviewed. They showed it over and over again. At least I looked okay and didn't come across as some old fool. I still couldn't see the Kenny Rogers connection apart from the hair colour (or lack thereof) and the beard.

I kept the TV on all day so that I could keep up with any new developments. Out in the lane, the police were stopping anyone who tried to get into the woods, a few locals were hanging around trying to see what was going on, and there were still far more reporters out there than anyone else. According to the news on TV, the police hadn't found anything untoward in the woods and still had no clue what had happened.

Later that day, I decided to go back into town to see if there was any more news from the locals. But there wasn't as many people in town. It just looked like a usual Wednesday afternoon. I made my way to the local pub, The Mackarbee Hotel. I often used to wonder why the pub was called Mackarbee instead of Mackarb, but it was probably because if it was called The Mackarb Hotel, it would attract too many idiots.

The pub was fuller than usual when I got there. I went to the bar and ordered a beer. While I was waiting, Graham came up beside me. He's a guy I've known for years. He's around my age and is divorced. He's been single for years. He works as a landscaper and gets plenty of work from the local people and the local businesses. He tends the grounds of the hotel at least one day a week and is often seen mowing the lawn in the beer garden out back. He was wearing his working clothes which are a khaki shirt and matching khaki shorts, so he'd probably just finished doing the hotel's gardens. "Did you hear about what happened in the woods?" he asked me.

"I've been watching the news all day and so far, they say no one knows."

"Well, one of the teens has been talking to his parents and they've told others." He nodded across the room. I turned and saw Rachel and Freddie Simmons talking to a large group of people. Rachel and Freddie were pub regulars but didn't usually command such a big audience. Graham said that the parents had said that their son, Douglas, who'd been with the gang in the woods, told them, and the police what happened, and they've been telling everyone."

"I take it no one has told the news crew."

"Hell no. It's a weird story and no one would believe them anyway. Even the police are having a hard time believing what he said."

I was instantly intrigued. "So, what did he say?"

The guy behind the bar brought me my beer. I paid for it, took a sip and then Graham and I sat on two empty stools at the bar, as he began to speak.

He said that the boys were all in the woods, talking and laughing when they suddenly heard a sound nearby, and it sounded like there was someone hiding nearby because they heard what sounded like a rustling of bushes and sticks snapping. It could have been just a dingo or a koala on the ground, but they didn't think so. They were convinced someone was out there with them. So, they started using bravado and yelling at the person to go away or they'd be sorry. Every time they yelled, the noises stopped. But when they went quiet, they started again, almost like someone was goading them.

They then began to dare each other to 'go and sort the person out' but none of them dared go alone. Then suddenly, Tyler Moore said he'd do it. He picked up a short, thick branch as a weapon. The others put on their torch apps so that they could see what was going to happen.

Tyler walked off holding the branch like a club as the noises continued. But once he disappeared into the dark beyond the bushes it all fell silent. He said it was so quiet that there wasn't even the usual sounds of the forest like plovers, owls, snakes, or small animals rummaging around on the floor. He said it was just dead silent and it spooked the hell out of all of them. They were scared. They said they hadn't realised until that moment how alone and isolated they were, and how dark and creepy it was in the woods.

They started calling out to Tyler but there was no response. They yelled for him to stop mucking about and that it wasn't funny anymore. But still there was nothing but stone-cold silence.

They were debating what to do, whether one of them should go and see where Tyler was, or whether two or more of them should go, what with safety in numbers and all that. But not one of them wanted to go and look. One of them even suggested they leave and get the hell out of the dark woods. But none of the others wanted to look as though they were scared even though they were all wide-eyed and terrified by this point.

They decided that they should all go and look in the bushes and that shining all their torch app lights together, they'd get a better look at where Tyler went and why he wasn't answering.

Just as they assembled themselves to move forward in a group, with one at the front and the others huddled behind him, there was a sudden noise. It was coming from a distance away, but it was loud, making them all jump. It was a scream. A blood curdling scream. All the boys screamed too in shock and fear.

Then the distant screaming stopped. The boys stopped screaming too. All they could hear was their own heavy breathing. It sounded like one of them was crying.

A sudden noise made them freeze. There was movement. Someone was in the woods, coming towards them. Closer and closer. The boys braced themselves for whatever or whoever was about to appear in front of them. Within seconds they saw the nearest bushes moving. Whoever it was, was about to reveal themselves.

A white-haired Tyler staggered out. His hair was white and standing on end. He screamed. The boys screamed. Tyler stopped screaming. The boys started sobbing. They had never been so scared in their whole lives and none of them knew what to do.

Tyler turned and lumbered away, his shoes dragging loudly on the dirt and gravel as though he had no strength to lift his feet as he walked. He trudged out of the woods, along the well-worn track they'd walked in on. They all stood and watched him go, sobbing the whole time.

Then there was silence. No more footsteps. They all stopped sobbing, holding their collective breath for what might happen next. They heard Tyler scream again, louder than before. A long, ear-splitting scream. Then silence. The boys all sobbed quietly to themselves. None of them wanted to stay in the woods any longer but they were afraid to leave. So, they stayed and cried, until they heard people and sirens. And then they ran as fast as they could.

When Graham finished telling me, I sat in silence for a few seconds. I'd been totally engrossed in the story. I wanted to know more. I wanted a happy ending. A happily ever after. But there couldn't be. Tyler was dead.

"And that's not all," Graham continued. "So far, the police can find no evidence of anything happening in the woods. All they found was the place where the kids were hanging out, and that was only because of the way they'd destroyed it and left loads of soft drink cans and other garbage strewn all over the place. They said it even looked like they'd been trying to start a fire. But there's nothing to show that anything bad happened there or that anyone was hiding in the bushes. Weird huh?"

I had to agree. It was weird indeed.

For the next few days, I stayed somewhat glued to the local news to find out more about what had gone on in the woods. There had to be some reasonable explanation as to what happened to Tyler Moore.

The locals naturally suspected that the other boys must have done something to him, but nothing could be proven, but that didn't stop all the disagreements going on between Teresa and David Moore and the parents of the other kids in The Octo Gang. It was becoming a regular occurrence to see them all screaming at each other in the street.

Tyler Moore had not been the most popular boy in the group. All the others teased him and called him Mary, for obvious reasons due to his name, so it was natural to assume that the others had something to do with his death in the woods, especially as they were the only ones there.

Two days later, I went into town and saw a huge argument going on between Tyler's parents and the parents of another boy, Douglas Simmons. Douglas was with his parents and Teresa and David Moore were yelling at them, but it was mostly Teresa.

"You know him and his friends did something to Tyler," she screamed.

"You don't know anything," Rachel Simmons spat back. "Someone killed him. Maybe it was you!"

Teresa screamed at Douglas. "What did you do? What did you and those other no-good ratbags do to my son? Just tell the truth! Tell me!" The usual mouthy Douglas Simmons just stood there silently and looked frightened.

Freddie Simmons tried to calm Teresa down. "Our son did nothing to your son. Stop yelling. You're making a spectacle of yourself."

Wow, I thought. That guy has no idea about women. You never tell an angry woman that she's behaving badly. It never ends well.

Teresa lunged at him, aiming at his face and gouging him with her long nails. The raking of his skin went from forehead to chin, narrowly missing his eyeballs. Blood immediately poured from the wound. Rachel Simmons lunged at Teresa, but the two men pulled them apart before they could do any more damage.

As the women struggled free, yelling and cursing at each other, a police car pulled up. Two policemen jumped out and handcuffed both women before forcing them both to sit down on two nearby benches. Freddie used his handkerchief to press against his face to stop the bleeding.

I kept walking after that, but I heard later that neither of the women were charged with anything but were ordered to stay away from each other. Or else.

It was a strange time for our little town. It was an unspoken us-and-them situation between the locals and the families of the group of teenage boys. Or at least the boys that were still alive.

No one knew for sure what had gone on in the woods that night, but they all blamed the teenagers. They MUST have done SOMETHING. What else could it be, they all said.

No one knew what had really happened or what had gone on in the woods that night, but the speculation about what had taken place was all anyone could talk about.

The parents of all the other boys were somewhat shunned by the rest of the locals, because they didn't know what to say to them anymore and only watched them with suspicion whenever they were seen in town, and they came into town less and less, clearly feeling uncomfortable and unwanted.

That's the problem when something bad happens and no one knows how it happened, people make up their own minds about what happened and who did it, which is understandable because we all want answers, even if it's the wrong one.

And it tore our usually close-knit, friendly town apart.

I personally had no opinion about what had happened. It was easy to blame the other boys, but what could they have done that scared another kid literally to death? It just wasn't logical.

And at this stage, no one knew of the horrors waiting in the woods for the rest of the boys.

No one knew that this was only the beginning.

Not yet.

# Unfinished Business

By the following Wednesday, a week later, the constant police presence and news reporter activity had calmed down. There were no people camped out in our lane anymore, although plenty of locals came to have a look and see if there was anything going on.

The police had left a caution tape across the entrance to the woods and so far, no one had crossed it. I wondered if it was respect or fear that kept them out. Quite a few locals had come up to sit on my veranda and chat when they saw me. At times there were several of them at once. It made me uncomfortable. I don't mind talking to people in town, but it seemed a bit intrusive to have half a dozen at a time sitting with me at my table on the veranda and sitting on my sofa swing.

The only person I welcomed was Isabel. I was sitting on the veranda having coffee on my own when she wandered down the lane late that afternoon, just as it was getting dark. She stood staring at the trees, her arms across her chest and her hands hugging her upper arms. She looked so beautiful standing there in the half light. Her long flowing skirt was blowing slightly in the breeze, and her white cotton blouse fit snugly to her slim figure. I enjoyed being able to get a good look at her, and she did look good. After a while she turned to walk away so I waved and called her name. "Hi!" She said, smiling, and waved back. I didn't want her to leave so I yelled, "Coffee?" She smiled again and came through the gate.

We went inside and I made us both a fresh cup. It turned out she liked her coffee the same way I do. Black. The way it's meant to be. We laughed and joked about how far removed from coffee the other crap is that people drink. "Since when did coffee contain caramel?" I laughed.

"Since they started making it with frothy milk instead of water. How do they have the audacity to still call it coffee?" She joked, but we both knew we were right. Coffee should be black. Nothing else should be added. We were the coffee experts.

We sat at the table on the veranda and chatted. She told me she used to be married but had divorced a few years ago and used the money from the divorce settlement to buy the house on Forrest Lane. Kids? Yes, she had kids, but two lived interstate and one lived abroad so she didn't see them much.

I told her about my wife dying years ago, which was why I moved to Mackarb. I wanted to get away to somewhere no one knew me. I'd never told anyone about Maggie so everyone in Mackarb thought I'd always been single, and I let them go on thinking that. "Please don't let them know my secret."

"Don't worry," she assured me. "It's none of their business. Did you and your wife have any children?"

"No. We'd only been married for three years and were both working and trying to save up as much money as we could before we started a family. She was going to quit her job to be a full-time mother and we were paying as much money as we could onto the mortgage to pay it off. We'd nearly done it too when we found out she was ill."

"I'm sorry."

"Don't be. It was a long time ago. I was lucky that I had my work to keep me busy, and settling into a new town here and a new area took a bit of getting used to. I'd been living up north all my life, so it was strange at first to live further south. But once I saw this town I knew it was where I wanted to be. There was just something relaxing about it."

"That's funny," she said smiling. "I felt the same way, especially when I saw this lane. I had no idea how busy it could get until last week though." Then she changed the subject. "So, what did you do for a living?"

"I was a computer programmer. I worked from home so I could live anywhere. I loved making computer programs, mostly for banks and other financial institutions, and I worked at night, so my days were free. How about you?"

"I worked similarly to you in a way. I did coding. I worked as a software engineer and developer. I worked from home too, but I worked days. The companies I worked for wanted me to be available during office hours. But I loved the work. It was easy, interesting and fun. I know that most people would find it boring, but I really liked it."

"But you don't do it anymore?"

"Sometimes I help out if one of my old companies needs help, but not much. I have plenty of other things to occupy my time. Plus, coding takes a lot of study to keep up with it."

"I know what you mean. I might not have been working during the day, but I was often sat here reading programming books and magazines."

Sitting on the veranda with Isabel felt good. She was great company and we had so much in common with both of us working with computers, both had been previously married, and we ended up as neighbours. We joked about it almost feeling like fate that we met. What were the chances of us both ending up on the same small street in the same small town?

She asked me my last name. I said Johnson. She started laughing. I didn't get the joke till she said that her name was also Johnson. It was her married name and she'd never changed it after her divorce. We laughed at the peculiarity of us having so much in common that we even shared the same surname. We figured you couldn't even make this stuff up.

"It's nice sitting here on your veranda," she said.

"I was just thinking the same thing." We smiled at each other then quickly looked away in embarrassment. I was extremely nervous. I had remained single since Maggie died, never looking romantically at another woman the whole time. I'd loved being with my wife so much I'd never been able to even contemplate being so content with anyone else.

But now here was Isabel who'd not only piqued my interest since the first time I'd laid eyes on her, but someone I was rapidly becoming extremely fond of. These feelings were completely out of my control, yet somehow I didn't mind. I just liked being with her for reasons I couldn't explain, not even to myself. I just loved everything about her; the way she smelled, her beautiful long, wavy, dark hair that was tinged with grey, her long flowing, skirts, and her elegant lace blouses and tops. She had a real gypsy look about her that I seemed to adore, and yet she looked the total opposite of my wife who always wore crisp, straight outfits that looked equally suitable for the office or leisure, and she always kept her hair neatly cropped short, and I'd loved everything about how she'd looked too.

Maggie's outer appearance had also complimented her inner no-nonsense attitude to people and life. In fact, her middle name could have been Practicality.

So, it seemed strange to be here now, loving the company of a woman who was the complete opposite in every way, down to her laid back and unhurried attitude to life.

Our 'moment' was suddenly broken by the sound of angry teenage voices. We looked up to see The Octo Gang coming down the lane with the torch apps on their cell phones lighting their way.

"I don't care. I'm sick of us all being accused of something we didn't do. Screw them!" one of them was yelling.

"This is crazy!" Another one complained loudly.

They were discussing the dangers of going back into the woods. Some of them thought it was dangerous. The others thought the only way to get suspicion off them was to go back into the woods and try and find out what happened.

They paused at the caution tape as they were speaking.

One of them said, "What if whoever did it is still in there?"

"The police didn't find anyone."

"Maybe they left but now they're back."

"Don't be stupid."

"What's stupid about it? They were there before. They could be there again."

"We don't even know if there was anyone in there. Ty could have just seen something that scared him."

"Oh, come on. No one's hair turns white like that over something they've seen. Someone scared him. And scared him to death. Literally."

"So," said another boy nervously, "are we going in, or aren't we?"

The boy who was clearly the dominant one of the group said, "Damn straight we are. Who's too scared?"

There was a few seconds of silence, then one quiet voice responded. "I'm not sure I want to go in there, but I don't want to stay out here alone either."

The dominant boy ducked under the caution tape. "Come on," he demanded, and one by one the other boys followed.

Their voices became harder to hear as they walked further into the woods, but I heard them say, "What are we going to do?"

"We're going to find whoever did this."

"How?"

"We'll just look for them. What else?"

"Let's start looking where Ty disappeared."

After that I couldn't hear what they were saying. Isabel and I looked at each other. She said, "I wouldn't go in there in the dark. Would you?"

"Hell no," I said, "But to be honest, until just now I wondered if it was the other boys who had something to do with what happened to their friend, but judging by their conversation I reckon they have no idea who did it."

"I was thinking the same thing," she said.

"Of course you were. We have the same name, and we live in the same street." We both laughed at my attempt at humour.

"Maybe they were saying it all for our benefit," she mused.

"I doubt they saw us sitting in the dark." I paused and then said, "Do you like beer?"

"Always," she said.

"Great. Come inside and I'll get a couple of cold ones out of the fridge, and we can put some lights on too."

She followed me inside, carrying the empty coffee cups that she put in the sink while I turned on a lamp and got the beers, opened them, and put them in stubby holders. "Cheers." We clinked bottle necks and went back outside. This time we sat on the sofa swing. It was dark outside. The only light was the soft lamp light coming through the front window. Isabel looked good sitting beside me with her long flowing skirt, long wavy hair, and her slim body. She looked good for her age.

I lifted my bottle and took a drink. As I lowered it back down, I thought I saw movement across the street. It was so dark in the lane that it was hard to see, but it looked like someone was standing out the front of Marvin's house. I glanced at Isabel. She was looking towards the woods.

I looked back across the street. The dark figure was also staring at the woods, or at least I could just about make out his silhouette facing towards the woods. He lifted his arms, his palms forwards. It looked like he was trying to push the trees using telekinesis. I glanced at Isabel again wondering if she saw the dark figure too, but her gaze was still locked on the entrance to the woods.

I looked across the street again and the figure was still standing there with his arms out and palms up, or at least that's what it looked like in the dark. I watched him for a few more seconds but it was so dark that when I stared too long, all the blackness of the house, the person and their dark clothes, all blended together and become harder to see. I blinked a couple of times to clear my vision. He lowered his arms slowly and walked down the side of the house and seemed to disappear in the shadows.

I was so transfixed by what I saw that when Isabel spoke I jumped. "What is it? Can you see something?" She was looking at me.

"I thought I saw someone."

"Where?"

"Just out there in front of the house."

Isabel leaned forward and stared into the darkness. "I don't see anyone."

"No, they've gone now."

"Who was it? One of the boys?"

"I don't think so. Maybe I'm seeing things." I didn't want to mention Marvin. So far, I didn't understand him myself and it seemed he was harder to spot than a Yeti. "Or maybe this is just getting too creepy with weird things going on in the woods and the teenagers in there again. I wish they hadn't gone in there." I sighed, wanting to change the subject so that my time with Isabel wasn't marred with anything unpleasant, so I said, "Let's not spoil our beers. Let's talk only about happy things."

"Agreed," she said, and we raised our bottles and clinked them.

"It's nice sitting here," said Isabel. "I don't know what it is, but I always feel relaxed when I'm with you."

"Yeah," I said smiling. "It must be the great company."

"It must be," said Isabel. "It's certainly not the creepy woods and the murders that relaxes me. But they have brought us together."

"Silver linings I guess," I said, tipping back my head and taking a drink of my beer.

Isabel smiled and was about to answer when loud shouting disturbed us. The voices were coming from the woods. We turned and looked in that direction, but all we could see was darkness and the voices were getting louder.

"Simmons! This is not funny!"

"Asshole! Where are you?"

"Get out here now or else!"

"Doug! DOUG!"

"Quiet! Everyone quiet! Let's see if we can hear him."

The woods instantly fell silent. Nothing was said for about half a minute then the shouting resumed.

"You're going to get it Simmons if you don't come out right NOW!"

"Where are you, you jerk!"

"Cut it out! Just quit hiding will you? THIS IS NOT FUNNY!"

"Simmons!" "Simmons!" "SIMMONS!" They all were taking turns at shouting his name.

Isabel turned to me. She looked worried. "Oh geez. Don't tell me another one of those boys has gone missing."

I didn't know what to say, so I said nothing.

The boys carried on shouting for their friend. I knew who the missing boy was. Douglas Simmons, son of Rachel and Freddie Simmons. I knew the family quite well, although we weren't constant companions, but I'd had a drink or two at the pub with Freddie and Rachel on the odd occasion, and we'd always spoken to each other at local gatherings. I'd watched their son Douglas grow up over the years. Rachel and Freddie had four kids and Douglas was their youngest.

Isabel had left her cell phone on the table. She went over and picked it up, putting her beer down in its place. "I'm going to call the police."

I thought she was being a bit premature. "No don't. He'll turn up. He's probably just hiding from them."

She frowned at me. "What if he isn't hiding? It's dangerous for them to be in there anyway." She tapped zero three times.

"Yes, I'd like to speak to the police." There was a slight pause and then she continued. "Hi, I live in Forrest Lane in Mackarb where a boy was murdered recently in the woods after he went in there with his friends at night. The same group of boys have gone into the woods again tonight and now one of their friends has gone missing in there."

Isabel walked out onto the lawn as she was speaking so I didn't hear much else of what she was saying but I could still hear the teenagers shouting for their friend. Their voices had changed, and they sounded more frightened than angry.

Their voices were also getting louder and within seconds they were all out on the street, standing outside the caution tape and shouting back into the woods, looking like they were too afraid to be in there themselves any longer. There was only six of the seven boys that had gone in there.

Isabel was still on the phone talking to the police. I went inside and made a call of my own. "Hello, Freddie? Yeah, I'm fine. Look, I don't know if you know or not, but the boys all went back into the woods tonight. Yep, all seven of them. Listen, the police have already been called and I don't know how to tell you this, but only six of them have come out and Douglas isn't with them, and they're scared Freddie... Freddie?" But it seemed he'd hung up. What seemed like only a minute later, he and Rachel came running down the lane, followed by two police cars with red and blue flashing lights.

The last time there was trouble in the lane, I mostly stayed away, but this time, as soon as I saw Freddie and Rachel, I went down to them, along with Isabel.

I knew it was going to be a long night. But for the sake of my friends, I hoped it would have a happy ending.

But it didn't.

# Everyone's a Suspect

It was a long night. The whole lane was filled with police cars, search teams, locals, and, of course, the media. I figured none of us were going to get any sleep, and I was right.

Sixteen year old Douglas Simmons was missing and no one could find him. The woods were searched and searched again. All the locals were hovering around Douglas's parents, Freddie and Rachel, but there was nothing that anyone could do, apart from Teresa and David Moore, who could empathise with them after they'd recently lost their own son Tyler in a similar way.

I stayed out there as long as I could, but the two cups of coffee and the beer that I'd had meant that I needed to go to the toilet. I turned to go back to my house to use my own bathroom.

The reporter who'd interviewed me last time came up to me again when she saw me going through my front gate. "Excuse me, Harold?" I turned and smiled when I recognised her. I even remembered her name, Susan Jackson. She had the same cameraman in tow. "Can you spare a few seconds to talk to me about what's happening here tonight?"

Before I could say, "Not really, you see I'm busting for a pee," the cameraman switched on his camera and pointed it directly at me. Things like that always take me off guard, and I was extra flustered because my bladder was full and because I knew that whatever I said would end up on national TV and maybe even international TV. I took a couple of deep breaths and tried to say only things that didn't really say anything. That way, nothing I said could be deemed wrong, or worse, sound stupid. So, I simply said, "Sadly it's the disappearance of another local teenager." She pointed her microphone at me as I spoke and then back at herself. "How did you know he was missing?"

"I saw seven boys go into the woods but only six came out. I don't know what happened in between that."

"What do the other boys say happened to him?"

"They don't know. From what I understand, he just vanished. I'm sure they'll find him because he has to be somewhere. Now if you'll excuse me I really, REALLY, need to go." I turned and walked away, not waiting for a response.

When I came out of the bathroom, Rachel Simmons was standing just inside my front door. "Sorry Harold. I just wondered if I can use your toilet?"

I went to her and held her hands. "Rachel, you can use anything you want. ANYTHING. You don't have to ask. Tell Freddie as well. Tea, coffee, toilet, somewhere to hide... you're welcome to it all." I shook her hands reassuringly then carried on. I'm never any good at dealing with death and grief, missing children, and other upsetting things. I never quite know what to say, so I try and say as little as possible.

I rejoined everyone outside. What I would have preferred was to go to bed and go to sleep, but that didn't seem like an option. Even though my presence wasn't helping anyone, it felt wrong to leave.

The search went on for hours, but Douglas wasn't found. The police and search teams decided that it would be best to start searching again when it was daylight. There was only a slither of moon and a lot of cloud making it impossible to see anything in the woods. Even the bright search lights could only penetrate a small area at a time because the trees with their huge branches cast such big shadows. So, at 2am they packed up and most of them left, except for a couple of police cars and the ever-present media people.

I went inside with Isabel and Freddie and Rachel. I don't think I've ever seen anyone as tense as Rachel was that night.

We all sat at my dinner table and drank coffee. Then we all had a beer. Rachel didn't say much the whole time and then she went and laid on the couch. Within a minute or two she was fast asleep, which surprised us all. How could a woman who was so wound up and tense, fall asleep so quickly? Or maybe being so wound up and tense for so long had exhausted her.

The three of us stayed at the table and all agreed that at least while Douglas was missing, there was still hope he'd be found unharmed. Freddie said that he and Rachel had forbade him to go anywhere near the woods and not to hang out with the other boys anymore. But being a teenager, he'd disobeyed his parents and done everything they'd told him not to do.

An hour later Rachel woke up, so I made breakfast for us all. It was only toast because I didn't have enough of anything else for so many people, but I did have a full loaf of bread and plenty of toppings, and we were all hungry. I also had enough orange juice and plenty of coffee. By the time we finished breakfast it was light outside and one by one all the cars arrived back in the lane and the search resumed.

It didn't take them long to find the missing boy. Weirdly, his body wasn't far into the woods, and was quite close to where he'd last been seen. No one could figure out why they hadn't found him the night before, especially considering his injuries made it obvious he'd been there for some time.

That morning, after Douglas's body had been taken away, and Freddie and Rachel were taken to the police station, the two police detectives that I'd spoken to when Tyler Moore died, John Simpson and Peter Norman, visited me again to ask what I knew and what I'd seen about Douglas Simmons.

Isabel was with me at the time, so they spoke to her too as she was the one who'd called the police, but neither of us could tell them anything. My mind wandered back to Marvin, standing in the dark outside his house, staring at the woods just before Douglas went missing, but I couldn't tell the police about that without them thinking I was crazy, or lying.

As Isabel and I sat on the front veranda with the two detectives. I looked at the house across the road where Marvin said he was staying. I wondered if he really was there. If he wasn't, the police would think I was completely nuts for talking about him.

I was exhausted from being up all night, I felt like I'd pass out if I didn't get some sleep soon, so once the police had gone, I said goodbye to Isabel and went inside. I put the TV on and laid on the couch. I watched the news channel to see what they were saying about last night. Just as before, they showed my interview over and over again. I soon fell asleep and didn't wake up till I heard someone knocking at the door.

I opened my eyes and saw that it was 3pm. Freddie was at the door. He came in and we had coffee, and he told me about his day, the worst day of his life. He said Rachel had gone to bed because she couldn't take what had happened and didn't want to talk to anyone.

He told me that he and Rachel had been taken to the police station that morning and questioned about Douglas's death. He said it was hard on Rachel to be questioned that way, as though they'd had something to do with it. Rachel also felt guilty for not knowing that Douglas had gone into the woods. She blamed herself for not calling him to check where he was. The other boys had also been taken to the police station and questioned.

He told me that his son, Douglas, had been found slumped against a tree, not far from where he went missing, and had been shot through the heart with an arrow, which had pinned him to the tree.

The police thought that someone must have stabbed him, removed the body, and then brought it back to put against the tree and shot an arrow through the stab wound to hide it. There could be no other explanation as to how he wasn't found straight away.

They also couldn't understand how the body was moved without leaving a trace on the ground. No soil seemed to have been disturbed and there were no drag marks. The teenage gang had obviously walked all over the area where Douglas had gone missing, so it was possible that they'd trampled any trace of drag marks. But there were none further away either, but there had been a lot of police searching the woods at the time because at that point they were searching for a missing boy, not a dead body.

But it was obvious that someone had taken Douglas from the scene and returned him later. How they'd done it was a mystery. So just like Tyler Moore, no one could explain Douglas Simmons' death.

Listening to Freddie made me feel unsettled. It was such a bizarre story. Tears ran down Freddie's face as he spoke, and I didn't know what to say to him, so I just listened as he poured everything out.

I sat there with him for over 2 hours. When he'd gone, I had a shower and as the water cascaded over my body, it felt like I was washing away the terrible story he'd just told me.

When I'd finished, dried myself slowly as the story of what happened to Douglas was still haunting my mind. I needed to get it out of my head. I put on my pyjamas, which are a t-shirt and a matching pair of shorts and settled down to watch TV and have something to eat. I needed to distract myself from everything that was happening, and everything I'd just heard. I left the front door closed so that no one else would disturb me, and no one did. I spent the next couple of hours watching 'stupid' TV then went to bed.

The next day, Friday, I wandered into town in the morning to hear the local gossip, glancing at Isabel's house as I went by, but there was no sign of life there. I found her on the green along with many other locals. I went and stood with her. She seemed happy to see me. My friend Stephen was there too.

"Hey look everyone!" Stephen announced loudly. "It's the Kenny Rogers of Mackarb." Everyone turned to look at me. Some smiled, many laughed. I stepped forward and stood in front of Stephen. "Don't ever do that again," I said in my sternest voice. His broad smile quickly disappeared from his face. I didn't like people calling me Kenny Rogers. It wasn't insulting. Just annoying. I knew people were calling me that on social media and that was bad enough, but I didn't want it in my personal life.

"Well, sorrreee," Stephen said sarcastically, holding up his palms in surrender.

"I just hate it so don't do it. Okay?" Then I changed the subject and turned to speak to everyone. "So, what's going on? Do we know any more about what's happening and who's doing it?"

"We were going to ask you," another man said.

I gave them a brief overview of what Freddie had told me. There were gasps and cringes from my eager audience.

Stephen asked me if I'd seen anything the night before when the boy went missing. "Didn't Isabel tell you?" I asked him, nodding toward her. I'd assumed, because she was already there that she'd have told them what little we'd seen.

"Tell me what?" Stephen asked.

"We were both there when the kids went into the woods and came out with one missing. That's all we saw. Isabel was the one who called the police."

"No, she hasn't said a thing," said Stephen. Then turning to Isabel he said, "Why didn't you tell us?"

Isabel looked embarrassed. "Because there's nothing to tell. We don't know anything about what went on."

"Hmmf," said Stephen sounding annoyed. "It seems weird that you kept quiet all the same." Then he changed the subject. "If you ask me, those boys know more than they're telling."

His remark started an angry debate, and everyone started talking at once.

"You don't know that for sure. There could have been anyone hiding in the woods."

"Who'd be hiding in there?"

"It could be a stranger."

"Why would a stranger want to kill those kids?"

"It could be one of us."

"Don't be ridiculous."

"No one likes those boys. They've done so many bad things."

"But no one wants them dead."

"Someone must. They're dead aren't they?"

"Seems to me they're killing each other just to cause more trouble."

"Oh, don't be so stupid. Why would anyone commit murder to upset other people?"

"Why do kids do anything? Because they're stupid."

"They're not just dead they were tortured. Who in their right mind would do that?"

"I think we've got a serial killer on the loose."

"There needs to be more than two murders for it to be serial."

"Oh, for goodness sake. Don't be so pedantic."

"A killer is a killer, and it could be anyone, or any one of us."

"Who the hell out of us would kill and torture kids like that?"

And on and on it went, with everyone getting angrier and angrier about it. I figured it was fear that was making them so mad. But no matter what it was, I'd heard enough so I left. I hadn't gone far when I heard Isabel say, "Wait up." I turned as she caught up with me. "Want to come to my place for a coffee?" She asked.

I was happy to be invited. "Sure. Love to." We crossed the road away from the green and started to make our way through the throngs of people standing on the footpaths talking, when we came across Freddie and David, the fathers of the two dead boys. They were yelling at the fathers of two of the other boys.

"It was your kid who was with mine when he died," yelled David. "He must have had something to do with it. I don't believe he's innocent. He's been a pain in everyone's arse around here and now he's involved with murdering my kid! Everyone knows what a dickhead your son is and he's always up to no good."

Matthew Drummond, the father of one of the other boys, Caleb, was furious and was clenching and unclenching his fists by his sides. "Our kids were always together so whatever my son did, SO DID YOURS you moron!"

David wasn't about to give up. "Whatever my son did he was goaded into by your idiot son! Everyone knows your son's an idiot!"

He was about to say more when Matthew Drummond launched himself forward, giving David an uppercut hard under his chin with one of his already clenched fists. David's head rocked back and he flew through the air backwards, hitting the pavement hard. The back of his head split open as it connected with the concrete with a loud thud, and blood pooled quickly. Some of the women watching knelt down to tend to the now unconscious David who's mouth also started to bleed. I heard someone on their phone calling for an ambulance. Matthew stormed off and no one dared stop him. He was livid.

"Come on," I said to Isabel, taking her hand and walking away. "We don't need any more drama."

I only meant to take her hand for an instant to get her away from there, but we continued to hold hands all the way to her house. We went inside to her kitchen and talked as she made coffee.

She said, "It's not really surprising that tempers are boiling over. I can't even get my head around what's happening here. It's all just so weird. It's not just that the boys died, it's how they died. I just don't get it."

"Me either. Something strange is going on here but I don't know what."

But I was determined to find out the next time I saw Marvin.

# Local Gossip

I stayed at Isabel's house having coffee for the next 3 hours after which, we ended up sitting on her front veranda with a couple of glasses of wine. Three times while we were sat there, reporters came up and asked if they could do an interview with us. We were feeling pretty mellow by that time so we said yes to them all, including Susan Jackson, and gave brief interviews saying, yet again, that we saw the teens go into the woods and come out with one of them missing but we couldn't say any more than that. The reporters were happy just to get such a small and useless amount of information and we supposed with all the 24-hour news coverage they must get short of things to show.

It would have been a lot more intimate sitting there with Isabel if all the police, and reporters, and all the other people were not in the lane. It was crowded and noisy. It would have also been more intimate if we hadn't talked non-stop about what had happened while we were alone with each other and spoken to the reporters when they arrived. But the murders were on everyone's mind all the time, including ours.

Over the next few days the police and all the news crews disappeared from the lane, but the caution tape remained across the entrance to the woods. Isabel and I still carried on seeing each other casually, which was something else on my mind because I wanted to take it further. But with everything that was going on, it didn't seem like the right time.

By Wednesday afternoon, the lane was empty. It was a cloudy day and there'd been some drizzle in the morning, which was a welcome break to all the hot, sunny days we'd been having. I went outside and stood on my front veranda, looking at the entrance to the woods. It used to give me a happy feeling to see so much natural environment, but now it looked trampled and ugly, especially with the caution tape still being there. And it wasn't just one piece of caution tape. It was wrapped around several trees several times across the entrance, high and low to try and stop people getting through it.

I wondered if I should go and knock on Marvin's door and ask him what was going on. He must know because he seemed to be part of it. He was with the white-haired teen when he passed out and he was at the woods before the second boy went missing. But what if I knocked and he didn't answer? Or what if he did answer? What would I say? I continued to contemplate it for what felt like quite a while when I heard a noise behind me.

The couple who live in the house beside Marvin's, Trevor and Jane, were walking towards me. "Are you thinking the same thing?" Asked Trevor.

"Maybe, if you're thinking shit this caution tape looks awful."

Jane laughed. "Well, that's part of it, but we were thinking that something really weird is going on and it's about time we all got together and talked about it."

"We?" I asked.

"Yes," said Trevor. "We as in all us folks who live in this lane. It's all happened right here yet none of us have been able to talk to each other. Why don't we all sit down together."

Jane jumped in, "We could all bring out some chairs and tables, and some drinks and nibbles, and sit in the road. It's about time we all talked."

I was about to say something when Isabel spoke. I was surprised to see her. I hadn't even seen her walking down the road. "I think that's a great idea. I'd love to know what you all think and what you saw. It will be interesting."

"It's settled then," said Jane. "Let's all go inside and get ready. We'll go tell the others and we'll all meet back out here as soon as we're ready. Oh, and everyone bring some mosquito coils or incense or something. We need to keep the mozzies away."

"Just one thing," I added. "When you say meet back out here, can it be further up the road, outside your place? I don't want to sit this close to the woods."

"Good idea," said Isabel. "If there's something in there, at least we'll see it coming. And we can prop up the tables so things don't slide off them. This little street might be only gently sloping but it'll be enough to make stuff slide off the tables."

Jane and Trevor laughed. "Yeah, let's not risk it, with things coming out of the woods AND sliding food and drinks."

We all parted and went to our homes. I had a shower then searched the pantry for nibbles. I had a couple of packets of potato chips, so I took them outside with me, as well as a cooler of cold beers. I put them on the veranda and carried my small veranda table out into the street. Trevor came out of his house at the same time, also carrying a table. His was a camping table. It turned out that the slight slope of our lane wasn't a big problem, so the tables didn't need much propping up and a few drink coasters did the trick.

By the time we all set everything up, it was 4 o'clock, Trevor joked that it was perfect timing for beer o'clock.

I sat next to Isabel. She had brought wine. We all drank our own drinks but shared the bowls of food on the tables. Someone had brought sausage rolls and someone else had brought pasties. It actually felt so good to relax in the company of my neighbours. We'd never all gotten together like this before. Jack and Doreen who lived next to Jane and Trevor and opposite Isabel were there, and Bruce and Sharon who lived in between Isabel and I.

"Before we start," said Bruce, "No one call Harold by his new name, Kenny Rogers. After seeing him confront Stephen the other day, it's clear he doesn't like it."

"You were there?" I asked.

"I reckon everyone was there that day. It seemed like the whole town was out."

He wasn't wrong. It was extremely busy in town that day. "Mine wasn't the biggest confrontation that day, it was when Mathew punched David and knocked him out cold."

There was laughter and a chorus of oh my Gods. "Does anyone know what happened to him? Is he okay?" I asked.

"Where the hell have you been hiding?" Asked Jack. "I thought that was part of the local gossip. He was in hospital with concussion for a couple of days, and then he was released. He threatened to press charges for GBH on Matthew but so far, he hasn't done it. I don't think he will because everyone is just so tense lately and we don't need any more drama than there already is."

"I haven't been out for the past few days." I said. "It's just too hard to get past everyone in the lane, especially the reporters. I don't know how much more they think I can tell them, yet they keep asking me every single time they see me. I've even started sitting on the back veranda sometimes just to avoid them."

"Yeah, you have you dog," said Bruce, smiling. "Not sitting alone though, are you?" He glanced at Isabel as he spoke. Everyone laughed.

Trevor said, "Damn you Bruce. Now you've let the cat out of the bag. These two think it's their secret. They think we don't see what goes on in our own street, but we always spot familiar faces in a crowd, flitting between their houses."

Isabel blushed visibly. "It's not a secret. How can it be with so many people around? And it's just coffee and drinks."

"Sure it is. SURE it is," said Jane.

I leaned towards Isabel. "Don't waste your time feeding the trolls."

"Trolls?" said Doreen, laughing.

"Oh, come ON," I pleaded. "This isn't what we came here to talk about."

"But it's damn interesting," said Sharon.

"It's damn no one else's business," said Isabel, half joking, half serious, which changed the subject immediately.

"Okay, so what do we all think is happening in our little lane?" asked Janet.

"If we knew that we'd have solved the crime," said Jack.

"Maybe," said Trevor, nodding at Marvin's house, "it's the ghost of old Jed come back."

"Yeah," said Bruce, "he was a weird old guy. No one really knew him, and his body laid there so long that his ghost is probably still here."

"Really, Bruce? That's all you've got?" asked Jane.

Bruce countered her objection straight away. "Hey, no one knows why Jed died and no one knows why those boys were killed."

"Oh, come on," said Jane, exasperatedly. "Jed was nearly 100 years old, so we know why he died, and those boys were murdered."

There was a brief pause. Isabel spoke quietly. "I don't like what's going on around here one bit. It's sad for the families of those boys and it creeps me out."

The conversation continued, but it was clear that no one had seen any more than Isabel and I had and none of us had a clue what was going on.

I didn't contribute much more because my mind had been distracted by Bruce's comment about the ghost of Jed. He was probably in the right direction with that, at least the part about Jed's house. Or maybe he was right. Was Marvin the ghost of Jed? Or was Marvin the ghost of Marvin? How could he live with no lights on in the house and without anyone seeing him?

It wasn't just the teenagers dying that was weird around here, it was Marvin. I was dying (no pun intended) to get to the bottom of who, or what, he was and what he had to do with everything. I just felt sure that he had something to do with it all.

It was hard biting my tongue and not asking anyone else about him, but clearly no one here had seen him.

I tried to forget about it for the time being and relax in the company of my neighbours, but my mind kept going back to Marvin and the house across the road.

I wanted to find out more about him.

I just didn't know when I'd see him again.

It turned out I was about to see him soon.

# Defeating Evil

I sat outside with my neighbours until around 10pm when we all decided to call it a night. It had been nice sitting in the middle of the road with everyone, despite the topic of conversation and despite all the mosquito coils we had to burn just to keep from getting bitten, although we all did receive a bite or two. And we were constantly interrupted by a police car stopping at the top of the lane every 20 minutes or so.

It was especially nice to spend more time with Isabel. Earlier that evening I'd intended to invite her back to my place for a drink, but by the time we all left I was exhausted, so I took back my table and chairs and my cooler and headed home alone.

I must have been more tired than I thought because the next morning I woke up to find it was 9 o'clock. I usually get up at 6. I vaguely remembered the alarm going off, but I must have pressed it and gone back to sleep. I figured it didn't matter anyway as I had no plans for the day.

I spent the day cleaning the house and mowing the lawn. By the time I put the lawn mower away it was almost completely dark, and I was exhausted. I went inside and went straight into the bathroom to have a shower. I knew I had to keep going because once I sat down, I doubted I'd get up again.

Freshly showered, I made a quick dinner that I ate in front of the TV. Once I'd finished eating, I started to fall asleep, but it was early, so I didn't want to go to bed yet.

I put the dirty dishes in the sink, made a cup of coffee, and took it out front to the veranda. It was nice to sit in the lane when it was quiet like it used to be, and because I hadn't been into town my head was free of the local gossip about everything. I sat and sipped my coffee and felt calm for the first time in a while.

I looked at the house across the road. It was in total darkness, no sign of life. I looked at the entrance to the woods. The caution tape was barely visible in the darkness, and I wished I couldn't see it at all. I wished none of this had happened. The darkness of the lane used to feel peaceful. Now it felt ominous. Something, or someone, could be lurking in the shadows. But despite that, I still enjoyed sitting outside at night.

I reluctantly finished drinking my coffee. I didn't want to go back inside yet so I sat there enjoying the quiet. All I could hear were the usual sounds of nature from the woods. When I'd first sat down it was raining lightly, and it was comforting to hear the patter on the roof and on the garden. By the time I finished my coffee the rain had stopped but water still dripped from the trees in the woods, and all the usual sounds of nature resumed.

I wasn't sure how long I sat there, but my peace and quiet was interrupted by voices. At first, they were distant but as they got nearer, I realised it was The Octo Gang. Oh no, not again, I thought to myself. But yes, again.

They were coming down the lane, all shouting bravely at their invisible foe in the woods.

"You've had it now!"

"We're coming to get you, you bastard!"

"You can't hide from us this time!"

"You're the one who's going to die!"

As they continued to yell, I noticed a soft light in the lane. I looked across the road and could just see Marvin looking out of one of the front windows. It was the only window where the blind was up. There was a faint, dim glow in the room behind him, so faint it was barely noticeable, but in the darkness of the lane, it was enough for me to be able to see him, or at least a silhouette that looked like him. His head was turned. He was watching the boys.

The teenagers continued to walk down the lane, shouting the whole time. They stopped a few feet from the entrance to the woods and fell silent. Marvin continued to watch them, but the boys were oblivious to Marvin. I felt nervous. I knew something bad was going to happen, but I had no idea what.

All my neighbours came out and stood in the road, looking at the group of six remaining teens. None of us knew what to do. The boys had stopped shouting and were talking quietly among themselves, then they continued on silently into the woods until they were consumed by the darkness.

I saw Marvin watching them go. Then he turned his head to look straight ahead, and although I couldn't see his face, I was sure he was looking right at me. Then the dim glow faded, and he too melted into the darkness. And if that wasn't unsettling enough, the blind that was up, was now down like the rest of them, even though I hadn't seen it move. It was as though it had just somehow magically appeared inside the window.

I went out into the street to talk to my neighbours.

"We should do something," said Jane. "We can't leave them in there all alone."

"Do you want to go in there?" asked Bruce.

"No," she said, "but we should do something, maybe call the police."

"Good idea," said Doreen. "I'll go call them now." She went back to her house.

Isabel spoke next. "That's all we can do for now except get out of the way before we get run over by the speeding police cars that will be here soon."

"Want to come and wait with me?" I asked her.

"Sure. Just let me go back and lock up and then I'll be right there."

We all walked back to our respective houses to wait. A couple of minutes later, Isabel arrived at my place, quickly followed by the first police car speeding into the lane.

Isabel and I sat together and watched the police get out of the car and start shouting for the boys to come out immediately. Within minutes two more cars arrived and one of them had a big spotlight that they shone into the woods.

"Come out now! Right now!" one of the policemen yelled through a megaphone. "I want all of you out of the woods immediately!"

It didn't take long for the boys to appear. They came out in a line, one by one.

I said to Isabel, "Did you see that? Only 5 came out."

"Oh damn. You're right," she said.

We continued to watch as the police spoke to the boys. At first it all seemed calm but suddenly the police raised their voices. "Where is he?"

"I told you," said one of the boys. "We thought he was with us."

"Caleb!" yelled another boy, facing back towards the woods. Then all the boys started yelling the same name. I knew the boy they were shouting to. Caleb Drummond. I was sure he was only 15 years old.

The police told them to be quiet. Three of the police got out their torches and headed into the woods. All the boys tried to follow them but were physically restrained by the remaining three policemen. They put the boys in the back of the police cars.

Isabel and I sat there watching without saying a word. We were sitting on the sofa swing. She took my hand and squeezed it. I squeezed hers back and we continued to sit holding hands, which, despite what was going on, felt good.

I don't know how long we waited but it wasn't long, maybe only 5 or 10 minutes and then one of the policemen came back out of the woods, almost stumbling as he walked. He spoke briefly to the others and then went back in.

One of the police turned his head and spoke into his radio handset that was attached to the shoulder of his uniform. He seemed to be having a tense conversation with someone. Then he ordered for the boys to be taken out of the cars and I could hear him demanding that they tell him what happened in the woods. It was clear that they were saying nothing happened, but the police weren't buying it.

Soon the lane was once again filled with more police, forensic teams, ambulances, and of course, the media, and a lot of lights that lit up the lane like it was daylight.

I turned to Isabel, who was still sitting silently beside me holding my hand. "Wine?"

"A whole bottle at least," she said. I went inside to pour a couple of glasses, glancing at the house across the road as I went. It still looked dark and abandoned, but for all I knew, Marvin could still be there looking out the front window, hiding in the darkness. It was an unnerving thought.

I sat with Isabel as we sipped our wine, and then we had another glass each, as we watched everything that was going on. Eventually, my usual reporter, Susan Jackson, with her glued-to-her-side cameraman, came up to the veranda.

"Harold, Isabel," she greeted us. "I'd like to say it's nice to see you both again, but under the circumstances, it seems inappropriate."

"Probably," I said. "But we only meet under extremely gruesome circumstances, don't we?"

She ignored my feeble attempt at humour. "Can you give me a few words about what's going on?" But before I could respond, a voice behind her made us all jump. "Please move away." It was one of the detectives that I'd spoken to before, John Simpson. He also had his usual partner with him, Peter Norman.

The reporter and her cameraman did as they were told.

"Detective Simpson," I greeted him.

"Hi Harold. Sorry we have to meet like this again, but this whole thing just keeps getting worse and I need to talk to you."

"Do you know Isabel?" I asked.

"Yes, hello, we've spoken before at your house at the end of the street."

"That's right," she said. "I remember you both."

"May I?" said Detective Simpson gesturing at one of the chairs at the small table and sitting down without waiting for a response. He sat facing us. Detective Norman did the same thing, and sat beside his partner, unzipping his notebook wallet and taking out his pen as usual.

"Do you two know what happened tonight?" Asked Detective Simpson.

Isabel and I glanced at each other and shook our heads. "All we know is that the boys went back into the woods, shouting and yelling about they were coming to get whoever was in there and make them pay for what they'd done to their friends." I told them.

"What time was this?"

"I'm not sure, but we reported them going in there straight away, so whatever time that triple zero call was made that's when they went in there."

"And there was no one else around? Just the boys?"

"Not that we could see, but it is pretty dark here without all your bright lights."

"Isabel, did you see anyone else?"

"No," she said. "We all came out when we heard the boys going into the woods, and we've been sitting here ever since. What's happened? Have they found the missing boy?"

Detective Simpson hesitated then said, "We found his body."

Isabel and I looked questioningly at each other. "But how?" I asked him. "We didn't hear anything. No screaming or yelling."

"That's what's strange." he said. "The boys are adamant that they were altogether until they came out into the street and realised their friend was missing. It's a story they're all sticking to."

"Why don't you believe them?"

"Because of the way we found the body."

I wasn't sure I wanted to know, but I needed to ask. "And how did you find him?"

"It looks like he's been viciously attacked."

"In what way?"

"I can't say at this point."

"Oh, come on. You can't tell us this much and then stop. We'll find out eventually."

"I know you will, but we don't want the media knowing about it."

"Oh, for goodness sake. I know the boys' families. I wouldn't tell the media anything. I haven't told them anything so far and I'm not about to start, and that's because their families have enough to cope with without all the details ending up on the news."

"I understand that, but one of your friends might tell them."

"I haven't told anyone anything. These people are grieving over what's happened. Why would I want to gossip about it? I'm not that callous. But if you don't tell me what's happened, I can't tell you if I saw or heard anything relevant."

The two detectives looked at each other and were silent for a few seconds. The younger one looked at the older one for direction.

"Okay," said Detective Simpson. "I'll tell you, but if this leaks out, I'll know it's come from one of you."

"Well thanks for the vote of confidence."

"I'm only telling you what we found in case you heard or saw something relevant." He took a deep breath as though unsure of how to continue. "We found the boy with his torso twisted."

Isabel and I exchanged a puzzled look. Detective Simpson continued after a slight pause. "He was on the ground with his chest facing up, and his hips facing down."

Isabel gasped. "What does that mean? How could that even happen?"

The detective took another deep breath. "This can happen when someone is hit by a speeding vehicle. But as no one has said they heard a vehicle, nor is it possible to drive one in the woods, we're guessing that's not how it happened."

"What else can it be?" I asked. Once again, I felt like I didn't really want to know the answer.

"Either something large hit him, or someone or some persons did it to him themselves. And there doesn't seem to have been any vehicle or tyre tracks near him, so we're left with the only other option."

"Oh for goodness sake," I said. "You can't really be thinking that the other boys did this to him?"

"And yet we are."

"No," said Isabel. "I can't believe they'd do that, or even think about doing it."

"They were the only ones there."

"But still..."

"This is the third death, and those boys were there every time. We don't believe that they're as innocent as they're saying."

"Look," I said. "Going around town upsetting people and damaging property is one thing, but murdering each other?"

"Right now what I really want to know is if you heard anything at all? Shouting? Screaming? A speeding vehicle? Anything at all will be helpful. Dying the way he did, we think he must have screamed, and loud, or the boys where shouting when they did it."

"Honestly, we heard nothing, so we have nothing to tell you," I told him. "It's like we already said, the boys went into the woods. We called you, they came out, but one was missing."

"Okay," said Detective Simpson resignedly. "But if you remember anything, call me." He reached into his top jacket pocket, pulled out a small card, and handed it to me. "Here's my number." Detective Norman closed his notebook, put his pen back in the wallet, and zipped it up. The two detectives then left.

I turned to Isabel once they'd gone. "Shall we finish the bottle?"

"Absolutely," she said. "I need a drink after that."

I picked up the two empty wine glasses and took them inside. As I came back out I glanced across the road. I saw someone standing in the dark at the side of Marvin's house. The police lights in the lane made it possible for me to just make out that it was actually Marvin. He was standing quite far back so he was hard to spot but there was no mistaking that it was him.

His head was tilted up ever so slightly and I knew that he was looking at me. We stared at each other for only 2 or 3 seconds, but it was 2 or 3 seconds of fear on my part. Although I was never sure why, seeing Marvin always put me on edge, probably because he was always lurking in the shadows.

As I watched him, he turned and disappeared into the dark around the back of the house.

"Are you okay?" Isabel asked looking from me to out into the street and back, trying to see what I was looking at.

"Yeah, I'm just taking it in, all this madness." I handed her a glass of wine and sat down beside her, but my mind was still on Marvin. Was he a serial killer? But how could he have done it all? He never seemed to be involved in what was going on… and yet he was.

I needed to find out more about him.

And I made up my mind right there and then that I would.

# Missing

I woke up the next morning when the alarm went off at 6 o'clock and the first thing I noticed was the babble from outside, so I knew that the lane was still full of people, not that I expected it to be any different.

I showered, changed and made myself some toast for breakfast and ate it in front of the TV while I watched the news which was all about the latest murder in Mackarb, which I knew it would be. It still seemed weird to see my own street and my house on TV and to recognise so many people.

They showed footage of the murdered boy's parents, Matthew and Mary Drummond, coming out of the police station. I noticed it was daylight when they emerged so they must have been there all night, although now that it was nearly summer, the sun was always up before 4am. Matthew and Mary both looked exhausted and had puffy faces as though they'd been crying a lot. It had been hard enough for me to hear what happened to their son Caleb, so I couldn't imagine what it was like for them.

The pictures on screen kept switching between previous footage from the other 2 murders and footage from last night and this morning. I even saw a brief flash of Isabel and I sitting on my front veranda. I had no idea they could film people so clearly in the dark. I sat there glued to the TV for a couple of hours before I could tear myself away. Even though everything I was watching was happening right here, it was still somehow fascinating to see it all on TV.

After I washed my dishes, I headed into town to see what was going on. It was hard getting through the throng of people in the lane. Reporters kept thrusting their microphones in my face and the police kept pushing them out of my way. One young police constable had to escort me to the end of the lane because they wouldn't leave me alone.

There were now solid barriers at the top of the lane. Four large concrete blocks had been placed on the road, one on each outer edge and two in the middle of the road. Two metal barriers were across the top of the blocks, their round metal legs slotted into holes in the concrete blocks. The police were guarding them to hold back the crowd that had gathered there. They weren't locals. I didn't recognise any of them. They were just a bunch of looky-loos.

As I approached with the young police constable, one of the other policemen lifted one end of one of the barriers and swung it open just enough for me to get through, then swung it back and dropped it back into its hole. I pushed my way through the crowd on the other side. A few people patted me on the back and shoulder as I made my way through them and said, "Hey Kenny. How Ya doing?" Ugh!

The town centre was already busy when I got there and there seemed to be just as many strangers as locals. I saw Stephen on the green standing with a small group that I recognised so I went to talk to them. They were busy discussing the latest events.

"It's got to be the rest of them. It's like they're doing sacrifices in the woods or something. Why else would they keep going in there?" Just then he noticed me approaching. "Hey it's Harold! Here's the guy you need to talk to. If anyone knows what's going on its him."

The whole group turned to look at me. "I'm just as much in the dark as you are," I told them. "Just because I live there doesn't mean they tell me anything. So, what's happening?"

"Oh, come on Harold," said Stephen. "You must have heard something. What are the police saying?"

"Look, I try and stay out of their way. I'm sick and tired of them all being outside my house. I had to have one of them escort me to the top of the lane just so that I could get away from the reporters. I did watch the news this morning though. Poor Matthew and Mary."

Just then, we heard a woman yelling. We all turned and saw Mary Drummond screaming at the mother of one of the other boys, Freida Newcomb, whose son Alex was one of The Octo Gang. "What did they do to him! What did your murdering little bastard and his mates do to my son?" Then POW! She punched Freida in the face so hard that poor Frieda went flying backwards, hitting her head hard on the pavement and was knocked out cold. Blood gushed from the back of her head.

Several of the locals quickly bent down to Freida. One woman took off her cotton jacket, folded it into a square, lifted up Freida's head, and pressed the back of it against the jacket to try and stem the bleeding. Mary stormed off.

Within seconds the sirens sounded, and soon the main square was full of police cars, an ambulance, and reporters. I turned to Stephen. "I guess the only good thing about them all being here is that they can respond swiftly when something else happens."

Before I realised it, Susan Jackson was in front of me with her microphone and cameraman. "Harold, what happened here?"

I could feel everyone looking at me. Even those who were looking at what was happening with Freida, turned their attention to me. I felt flustered. "Well, as you can imagine, with everything that's happened here, the kids' parents are worried and sometimes that can cause accidents."

"From what I understand, it was one of the parents assaulting another." She pointed the microphone at her own face as she spoke and then pointed it back at me.

"Their frustration is understandable with everything that's going on. You have to understand that this is a terrible thing that's happening in our town. It's hard on everyone. Excuse me." I walked away before she could ask me anything else.

I was so sick and tired of the whole thing. The teens being murdered was bad enough, but the police and the reporters and the rubberneckers were all too much to bear.

It was mid-morning, and I knew that the pub would be open so I headed there. I wasn't a morning drinker, but I needed a quiet place to escape. But as soon as I stepped through the door of the lounge bar, I saw it wasn't the quiet place I was expecting. It was full of reporters. I recognised some of them from outside my house. I closed the door and headed to the sports bar instead. There were only a couple of locals sitting at the bar and no one else. I went in and asked for an orange juice.

"Hey Harold," said one of the men sitting at the bar. I couldn't remember his name.

"What's going on with all the media people in the lounge?" I asked him.

"Haven't you heard?" he said with a heavy sigh. "They're staying here now. Seems they're hoping there'll be more deaths. Morbid buggers."

"No, I hadn't heard. But that's probably because I've been trying to avoid it all."

"I'm not surprised with you living right in the middle of it all. Can't turn on the TV lately without seeing you on the news. And what's going on with you and Miss Johnson? I keep seeing the two of you together."

I felt annoyed that he mentioned it. It was no one else's business. I tried to sound casual in my reply. "Oh not much really. Nothing brings people together more than a shared tragedy and we're two single people trapped on the same small street, surrounded by crazy people and crazy stuff."

"I know what you mean," he said slowly, and I could tell that his mind had drifted away from our conversation. I walked away and sat at a table at the back of the room.

As I drank my juice I decided the best thing to do was to stock up on groceries, head home, and stay there.

It was a good plan. I bought two bags of groceries on the way home and my plan worked for the next few days. I stayed in my house and didn't see anyone at all. Until Isabel knocked at my door.

"I just thought I'd come and see how you're doing," she said.

I was glad to see her. I'd been thinking of getting in touch and asking if she wanted to come over for a drink. And now here she was on a Friday night, casually dropping by.

I immediately invited her in and opened two beers without even asking if she wanted one. We took them outside and sat at the table on the front verandah.

We'd only just sat down when I heard a voice saying, "Hey neighbours!" It was Jack with his wife Doreen. They lived in the house at the top of the lane opposite Isabel's. They were coming up the front path, each carrying an open beer.

I was pleased to see them but also a little annoyed because I wanted to spend some time with Isabel alone. We all greeted each other, and they sat at the table with us.

Jack looked out at the lane and said to Isabel, "We saw you head this way, so we figured we'd come and join you for a drink."

"How did you know we'd be drinking?" I asked.

Jack laughed. "Oh come on. We've seen the two of you sitting here several times on the news, it's now known nationally that the two of you drink together."

Isabel smiled and said, "That's not good."

Doreen said, "Don't worry. The lane's quiet again now that the police and reporters have gone. Let's hope nothing else is going to happen. Do the police even know what's going on or who's doing it?"

They all turned and looked at me. I shrugged and said, "How would I know?"

Jack said, "You live the nearest."

I laughed. "So what?"

"Well you must hear things. The police are outside here all the time. Don't you hear what they're saying?"

"From here? All I can hear is an ongoing babble of voices, and to be honest, I never pay attention. I'm always more worried about the things I hear from the woods."

That started a whole discussion about the murders. Jack and Doreen said that most of the locals now think that it's not The Octo Gang doing it. But who else could it be? All the parents now feared for their kids, and not just the parents of the remaining teens.

We all agreed that no matter what was going on and no matter who was doing it, our quiet, little town was changed forever, and there would probably be a book and movie about what had happened once it was all over. They laughed and joked about which movie star would play each of us.

"We'll all be famous," said Doreen.

Isabel grimaced. "Yeah but for the wrong reason."

Jack looked at me and said, "You're already famous. It seems millions already know about you, Kenny."

It was true. I already seemed to be well known because of my apparent similarity to Kenny Rogers. I told them that I'd already started receiving fan mail. My crazy fans even address the envelopes to Kenny Rogers Lookalike, Forrest Lane, Mackarb. They all had a good laugh about it and said it's also the big local joke.

But the laughter we were sharing was only surface deep. Mackarb was now a town of frightened people. No one trusted strangers anymore and we were all tired of the sick-minded people who visited every day, wanting to visit the town where all the grisly murders were happening.

The police had erected barriers at the top of the lane, patrolled it 24/7 now, and wouldn't let anyone enter. They hadn't barricaded the woods though. Only caution taped it. Probably because no one wanted to go in there.

*       *       *

The next day, Saturday, I walked down to the entrance of the woods in the late afternoon. It somehow looked different, dark and sinister, but I wasn't sure how much of that was my own imagination.

Before the murders, I would sit on my verandah at night, listening to all the sounds from the woods – frogs, night birds, sticks snapping, bushes rustling – and enjoy the familiarity.

Now, whenever I heard a noise from inside the woods, I wondered who was in there and what they were up to, and wondered if it was Marvin. I still hadn't seen him.

I looked towards his house as I thought of him, and there he was, standing by the side of the house, watching me. It made me jump. I hoped he hadn't noticed but the sight of him startled me. My heart raced. I told myself to calm down. He was just my neighbour, and he wasn't doing anything wrong.

But I knew that wasn't true. He wasn't JUST my neighbour. He was a strange man (Alien? Magician? Nutcase? Homicidal Maniac? All of the above?) who had done some really weird things and always just before a death occurred, or AS a death occurred. It was Marvin at the glowing windows when the white-haired boy died (or at least when he passed out in the street just before he died.)

Marvin was also there the other night too, just before another boy went missing. I'd been dying (pardon the pun) to find out more about this strange little man.

In my imagination, the next time I saw him I'd walk straight up to him and ask what's going on. Yet now that he was here, silently watching me, I was nervous. It was probably because he caught me off-guard, and probably because seeing anyone watching you is creepy.

But this was my chance, so I took it.

"Marvin." I walked towards him as I spoke. His demeanour didn't change. He just stood there watching me, so I continued. "I was hoping I'd run into you once everything calmed down."

I stopped within six feet of him. He stood silently, saying nothing, and giving no indication of whether he wanted to speak to me or not. Geez it was unnerving.

His silence gave me no option but to go on.

"What's going on with you?" I tried to keep my voice positive so that he wouldn't think I was accusing him of anything, even though I was.

Marvin didn't answer, just stared at me with the same blank expression. He was doing that thing he did before, staring straight into my eyes.

"Marvin?" I prompted.

He finally spoke in that flat unemotional tone that I'd heard before. "I don't understand the question."

"I keep seeing you every time something happens in the woods, yet no one else sees you or even knows you're here. They all think this is still an empty house."

Without missing a beat Marvin said, "People only see what they want to see. A stranger living in their street would be too much for them right now so they don't see me."

I thought the reason for his not wanting to be seen was more likely to do with him being a suspect if the police and the locals found out he was here, but I didn't want to say so. Instead, I said, "What do you know about the murders?"

Again, without missing a beat he said, "It's Karma."

His answer took me by surprise. I was at a loss of how to respond. But I didn't have to because Marvin continued. "The teenagers have done so much damage to people's property, and their emotions. It's said they even killed a boy, yet they go unpunished for everything they do, and now they're destroying the woods. Maybe nature is taking revenge. Or maybe someone is doing what others can't do yet but wish they could." He spoke in an unemotional, monotone voice all the time, all the while looking me straight in the eyes.

I remembered that they always say that if someone can't look you in the eye when they're talking, it's because they're lying. If that was true, then Marvin must be the most honest person in the world.

But what he was saying sounded ridiculous, but clearly, he believed it. "Are you saying that people wanted those awful things to happen?"

Marvin continued to stare into my eyes. I kept trying to look away, but I couldn't. He said, "People use their speech to hide their evil thoughts, and only say what they think others want to hear. They are all hypocrites and think they can hide how they feel. But deep down, none of the local people are sorry that the teenagers are finally getting what they deserve."

Once again, I had no idea how to respond, but what I really wanted to ask him about was his own contributions to what had happened.

Just as I opened my mouth, Marvin interrupted me. "Your girlfriend is looking for you." His eyes moved past me towards my house. I turned and saw Isabel arriving at my gate.

She turned and waved as she saw me. "Finally." I thought to myself, "Someone else has seen Marvin." But when I turned back to look at him, he was gone.

Isabel crossed the road towards me. "What are you doing over here?"

"Did you see him?"

"Who?" She looked totally confused and I suddenly realised that if I tried to tell her about Marvin, I'd sound crazy, so I said "I was by the woods when I thought I saw someone over here."

"At this old place? No one's lived here for years, have they?"

"I guess not," I said, and then changed the subject quickly. "Must be senility creeping in. Come on." I held her hand and walked her back to my place. "I've got a bottle of cold wine in the fridge. Let's open it."

Once again, I was the only person to see Marvin. It was eerie. Damn eerie.

I thought it was going to be a romantic evening for two when Isabel and I sat on my veranda drinking wine on that warm Saturday night.

It had been over a week since anything bad happened in the woods and the police had been doing an excellent job of keeping everyone out of the lane.

It was dark now and we were alone. Isabel and I were sitting on the sofa swing together. As she was speaking I turned towards her. She turned towards me and smiled. I leaned forward and kissed her. She kissed me back. Our lips stayed together, and we both inched closer. I tried to put my arm around her, but it was clumsy because I still had a glass of wine in my other hand, but I wasn't going to let it spoil our intimacy.

But the moment was broken when we heard whispering voices. We broke our embrace and looked towards the entrance to the woods which seemed to be where the voices were coming from.

We both stared silently, trying to hear what the voices were saying. It sounded like ghostly whisperings in an old graveyard as though the dead were talking. The sound made the hairs on the back of my neck stand on end.

Isabel took my hand and whispered, "This is weird. What's happening?"

"I have no idea." I could tell Isabel was scared. So was I. No one had come down the lane so where were the voices coming from and what were they up to? At first it had sounded like the whispering voices were coming from the woods, but now I wasn't so sure.

Isabel squeezed my hand and whispered, "Why would anyone go into the woods at night after everything that's happened?"

"I don't think they're in the woods." I said.

Both Isabel and I began to turn our heads slightly left and right as though trying to pick up a better audio signal. It must have worked because I suddenly realised where the voices were coming from. "Over there," I said, pointing to Marvin's house.

"It looks empty," Isabel said.

"Not in there. At the back." We both strained to hear. "I think you're right," she said.

We continued to listen. The whispering eventually became louder, not just because when people whisper they get louder without realising it, but because they were getting closer, coming down the side of the house next to the woods.

They were approaching slowly, and it was so dark back there that we couldn't see a thing. But the voices eventually became familiar, and Isabel loosened her grip on my hand. "I don't believe it," she said in a soft voice. "It's the teens, isn't it?"

"Yep, it sounds like it."

Soon we could see their dark shadows at the side of the house, and it seemed they'd forgotten the need to whisper. I could hear them saying, that they were going to find the bastard who had killed their friends once and for all. It was pretty much what they'd said before, except this time they all sounded scared, which made me wonder if they were completely stupid. There was someone or something in the woods killing them one by one, and they thought that the best thing to do would be to go back in and let them kill again.

"Remember, we need to stay together no matter what," I heard one of them say. Wow, what a great plan.

Isabel whispered, "Should we do something? We need to stop them."

Before I could say anything, the group of teens bolted into the woods shouting, "Get him!" as they went.

Isabel said, "Oh no. What do we do now?"

"Don't ask me. I'm not going in after them."

Just as I said that we heard the sound of a car approaching, its headlights lighting up the entrance to the woods. It was a police car from the top of the lane.

They turned off their engine and got out, leaving the headlights on. The two young constables looked around and saw Isabel and I sitting on the veranda. Damn those headlights. We'd been almost invisible until then.

One of the constables came to the gate. "What was that?" He shouted.

Isabel got up and went to talk to him. I couldn't hear what she said, but she pointed at Marvin's house and then at the woods.

She came back up to the veranda and the two constables set off into the woods with torches.

"So..." I said to Isabel. "Five teenagers go into the woods. How many are going to come out? I'm guessing four."

"Don't even joke about it," she said half laughing. "The police have gone straight in after them so they should find them all still in one piece. Oh damn," she said, frowning. "I phrased that badly. I meant all okay."

We waited a while, not saying anything, just staring out into the street and wondering what would happen next.

Eventually we heard voices and footsteps coming from the woods. The sounds were coming closer and closer until eventually they came out into the street, one policeman, followed by several teens, and finally the other policeman protecting the rear of the group.

Isabel and I looked at each other and by the worried look on her face I could tell that she'd counted the teens too. There were only four of them.

I heard one of the teens say, "Hey, where's Al?" The whole group started looking at each other as though one of them might actually turn out to be Al.

The policeman who'd led the group out turned to the other one and said, "What happened?"

"I don't know," he said, looking back towards the entrance to the woods as though Al might suddenly, miraculously appear. "I was behind them the whole way. I swear no one left the group."

"Well clearly one of them did," said the first one and went straight to the police car and called for back up to find a missing teen.

It only took a few minutes for two other cars to arrive, each carrying two more police. The policeman who'd led the group out quickly briefed the four new arrivals. Three of them went into the woods with him and the other stayed with the teens. The policeman who'd walked with the group at the rear stayed out on the street too and I wondered if it was because they didn't trust him anymore.

"Come on," I said, taking Isabel's hand and leading her out into the street. "Let's find out what's going on."

"Is everyone okay?" I asked once we were out on the street. "Who's missing?"

"Alex Newcomb," said the rear policeman. "Did you see him at all?"

"Sorry, I didn't see anything. Just you guys. How did he go missing?"

"That's what we can't figure out," said the rear policeman. "We found all five of them and I was behind them the whole way out. Yet by the time we got out here he was gone. I've wracked my brain trying to figure out when he disappeared, but I just don't remember."

"He wouldn't have gone on his own," said one of the teens who I was sure was called Tracey Nolan.

"We all agreed it wasn't safe to split up. He wouldn't have gone." He seemed distraught. So did the others.

"Tracey." I said, and paused, hoping he'd look at me for confirmation that I'd got his name right. He did, so I carried on. "Did any of you see him leave the group?"

"He wouldn't have," wailed Tracey. "That's the thing, but no one's listening to us. Al would never have left on his own. NEVER! We're not stupid. We know how dangerous it is for us to be alone in the woods after what's already happened."

"It's dangerous to go in the woods AT ALL whether you're in a group or not," I told him.

"Well, we know that now," he said, emphasising the word 'now' as though that made them seem less stupid.

The rear policeman berated him. "You kids need to stay out of the woods. Period!"

The boys all dropped their gaze to the ground. I spoke to them about their friend again. "Whether Alex went missing willingly or unwillingly doesn't matter. The only thing that matters right now is that he DID go missing and you four were right there with him. Did you see anything or hear anything? Anything at all?"

The teens all shuffled their feet and stared at their shoes. It was strange how they did everything in unison as though they were all operating from one collective mind. I wondered if all teens were like that. Had we all been the same when we were teenagers? Probably. It was hard to remember things that happened fifty years ago. Yeesh! Was it really that long ago?

I brought my mind back to the present. Isabel was talking to the other policeman who was talking notes. She was telling him how we heard, then saw the teens coming from the back of Marvin's house and run into the woods. He asked her the address of the house behind Marvins. Isabel didn't know but the policeman said he'd find out and contact them to see if the teens had gone through their yard as well. It made sense that they probably went through one property to climb the back fence into another. But I couldn't see how that information would help them.

My gaze shifted idly to Marvin's house as they were talking, and I got such a fright that my heart suddenly hammered in my chest.

In the darkness of the backyard, just back from the house a bit, on the side between the house and the woods, were two red glowing eyes. They looked like the red dots you get from laser pointers. They were moving slightly as though they were still attached to someone's face and looking left to right.

I looked around at the others. No one was looking in the same direction as me. No one was seeing the red glowing eyes.

I quickly looked back at the eyes, afraid of what they might have done while I wasn't looking. They kept up their slight movement. I nervously wiped my mouth with my hand and realised I was shaking. I put it down immediately so that no one else would see it.

Was that Marvin over there? If so, what did he have on his eyes to make them glow deep red like that?

I had seen in movies that if someone is wearing night vision goggles, others can see the red glow from them. Or was it green? Everything looked green through them, so they must glow green as well. Mustn't they? The more I thought about it the more sure I was that it was green. So, what made eyes glow red in the dark? Or if it was Marvin, was it his actual eyes that glowed red? But I'd seen Marvin in the dark before and his eyes never glowed red. But that didn't mean they weren't doing so now. The thought made me uneasy.

I told myself that if I was a brave person, I'd walk straight over there to see what was going on. But I wasn't a brave person, or, more correctly, I wasn't a stupid person, because only a stupid person would wander into a dark place all alone to see why two eyes were glowing red. There was already one person missing and if the eyes had anything to do with it, then I didn't want to be their second victim.

"Have you seen something?" The sound of the rear policeman's voice made me jump. I hadn't realised how lost I was in my own thoughts until he spoke.

I looked at him for a split second and then back at the eyes, which turned and walked to the back of the house and disappeared.

"No," I said, "Just wishing I could tell you something that might help." I tried to sound as normal as possible, but my heart was racing, and I was scared. Those creepy, glowing eyes were like something out of a horror movie.

I continued to stare into the darkness, just in case the glowing red eyes returned. After a few minutes, I pulled my gaze away and listened to what was going on instead.

I kept glancing at Marvin's backyard, but no more glowing eyes appeared. I soon started to doubt myself. Could it have been two red dots from two laser pointers? Was it kids making a practical joke? Did I really see the dots at all? Were my own eyes playing tricks on me?

Either they were glowing eyes, or laser dots, or I was crazy.

Each of those scenarios could be true.

But I'd probably never know the truth.

# Found

The police didn't find the missing teen, even though they searched all night. Young Alex Newcomb was gone, and no one knew where he was.

His father, Anthony, was notified after the first small search team failed to find him.

More police and tracker dogs were brought in, but he still couldn't be found. I could see all the media people gathering at the top of the lane, but this time the police were keeping them away, for which I was grateful, because I was still receiving mail from crazy old ladies and I didn't want any more, so the less I was seen on TV, the better.

It was almost daylight by the time I went to bed. I'd stayed outside for hours with poor Anthony. His son Alex was missing, and there was nothing anyone could do to help him. His wife, Frieda, hadn't come with him because, he told me, she was still in hospital with terrible concussion and stitches in her head after the punch to the face from Mary Drummond. I'd seen at the time that Frieda's head had split open and gushed blood when she fell backwards and hit the ground, but I wasn't aware until now how bad her injuries were.

Anthony said that he hadn't told Frieda that Alex was missing because there was no point worrying her over something she could do nothing about. He felt it was better to wait until tomorrow when, hopefully, Alex would have been found by then.

"Do you know what really makes me mad right now?" asked Anthony. "And I don't even know why it should bother me when I've got much bigger problems. My son is missing, and I don't even know if he's dead or alive, and my wife is in hospital with severe injuries, yet what's really rankling me right now is how dare Mary Drummond accuse our son of having something to do with her son's murder. And now what I keep thinking about is wanting to say to her 'See? It had nothing to do with my son because something's happened to him now too. See? You were wrong.'"

I put my arm around his shoulder and said, "Our brains seem to work in strange ways sometimes. Maybe yours is just keeping you thinking about something less important to stop you dwelling too much on what's going on now."

"Maybe," he said, and I felt his shoulders ease somewhat. "I hope that's what it is otherwise I'm going insane."

I stayed with him as long as I could that night, but I couldn't help him. The other neighbours had all come out too. I was exhausted, so I said goodnight to Isabel and went to bed just as it was coming fully light.

I didn't get up till almost midday. I felt ravenous and realised I hadn't eaten for nearly seventeen hours, so once I'd showered and dressed I made myself a cooked breakfast (lunch?) and watched the news while I ate it. There were still a couple of police cars in the lane and a few policemen and women, so I guessed they hadn't found young Alex yet, and I was right.

Nearly all the news was about another missing boy in Mackarb, and they were rehashing everything that had happened before.

By the time I'd finished breakfast and washed the dishes, everyone was gone from out front. I was just making myself a second cup of coffee when there was a knock at the door. It was Detective John Simpson and his usual sidekick, young Detective Peter Norman. I invited them in, made us all coffee, and sat at the kitchen table with them.

They asked me the usual questions about what did I see and what did I hear, but as usual I had nothing to tell them. I hadn't even seen the teens since the last murder, until last night, of course.

I asked them about the search for Alex and they said it was unsuccessful.

"There is just no sign of him at all," said Detective Simpson. "Even the dogs and the Delta team couldn't find any trace of him, apart from when he was with the others, and then 'poof!' it's like he vanished into thin air. We even tried widening the search several times, but there wasn't a trace."

"So what now? Is that it? Are you just going to stop looking?"

"No, of course not. It's just a waste of time to keep doing what we're doing and searching in the same places. We'll do some arial searches and make door to door enquiries. Plus, we've still got the rest of the group of boys that we're trying to sweat answers out of."

None of it sounded like they were hopeful of finding young Alex alive, or finding him at all.

Later that afternoon, I was sitting on my verandah having a cup of coffee when I saw movement out of the corner of my eye. I tipped up my cup to drink the last mouthful of coffee, and as I lowered it again I could have sworn I saw someone disappear into the woods, and it looked like Marvin.

I sat there for a couple of seconds trying to decide whether I'd actually seen him or not. And if it was him, what was he up to now?

I decided that this could be my chance to find out. I put my cup down, picked up my phone, and headed straight for the woods.

At the entrance I hesitated, but only briefly. I hadn't been in the woods in a long time, and now it felt strange (and scary) to go in there after the murders had happened, and to be following the man who I thought had done it. Luckily, or unluckily, depending on which way you looked at it, I didn't have time to think about whether what I was doing was smart move or not, so I just kept going.

But this was it. I had to go in if I wanted to find out what was going on, 'Or if you want to die too,' a voice inside my head warned me.

I walked forwards, unsure of which way to go, but the most worn path was the one straight ahead, not the ones diagonally either side of it, or the paths going immediately left and right of the entrance. And every time I saw people go in here, both teens and police, they always seemed to walk straight ahead.

But Marvin could have gone in any direction.

Suddenly, as though on cue, a stick snapped somewhere up ahead to my left up the diagonal path, so I headed that way.

The forest had always seemed like a pleasant place to be, until now. As I walked, I felt like I was going closer to danger. My fight or flight response was on high alert, or more correctly, my flight response was on high alert. I was so tense that I knew the slightest hint of trouble and I was out of there.

It was years since I'd run anywhere, but adrenalin is a marvellous motivator.

Why the hell was I doing this anyway? Was I really this desperate to find out what Marvin was up to? I wasn't even sure it was him that I saw, or if I actually saw someone at all.

Crack! Another stick snapped to my left. I turned my head in that direction almost simultaneously. I stood and stared for at least 30 seconds, but no other sound came.

All I could hear was my own heavy breathing. The question was, should I go off the path and walk in that direction, deep into the woods, or keep going? The sound had seemed to come from a bit further ahead, so I stayed on the path for the time being.

After a couple of minutes, I heard another sound to my left, but this time it seemed much closer. It wasn't a stick snapping. It was much more alarming than that. It sounded like a man coughing. Just one cough, but it was enough to literally stop me in my tracks and make my heart start to hammer.

My mind tried to calm me down by thinking that maybe it wasn't a cough at all, just something that sounded like a cough. Just like a cat bird is so called because it sounds like a cat crying, perhaps I'd just heard a bird that sounds like it's coughing. I desperately wanted to believe that. But I didn't. I was sure I'd heard some ONE, not some THING.

I turned all around looking for anything that might have made the coughing sound, and hoping that it wasn't a person, and as I looked at my surroundings, I had the sudden sinking realisation of how far I'd walked and how isolated I was. I knew how large these woods were and I was a small dot within them.

The woods began at the end of Forrest Lane and opened out immediately on both sides, wider and wider, sharing boundaries with large properties, many properties being well over 50 acres.

The woods went forward for several kilometres slowly rising upwards and ending at a cliff.

That's why it was easy to keep people out of here. Right then it was a reason to worry, especially because I thought I might be alone in here with a mad man.

As I turned in the direction of the cough, I thought I saw someone quickly duck behind a tree. It was one quick step in less than a second, but I saw it. Or did I? As I stared and saw nothing but the trees and bushes, I immediately doubted that I'd seen anything in the first place. It had happened so fast. Maybe it was a trick of the eye and I only thought I saw something (or someone) move. Or maybe I did see something, but it was a swaying branch. "There is no breeze." My logical mind was right. It takes a lot of wind to move a branch and the air was still.

But I was sure I'd seen someone. And the weirdest thing was that it didn't look like Marvin. Even though I'd seen them only fleetingly and from a distance, it looked like someone else. Marvin had dark hair, this person looked blonde. Marvin was middle aged. This person moved like a young person.

Alex Newcombe was young and blonde. That thought made me feel better. I was still terrified, but at least now I had a smidgen of hope that it wasn't a madman that was in the woods with me.

Had I just found Alex? Had he been hiding here the whole time? But why would anyone hide out here for so long, and for no reason? No wonder the police couldn't find him if he kept running away. But then again, they said there was no trace of Alex.

Even the tracker dogs couldn't pick up his scent except for where they knew he'd already been.

I knew that I should go and see if it was Alex, and I also knew that it would start getting dark soon and I didn't want to be stuck out here. It was already darker in here with all the trees. But there was no way I could leave without at least having a quick look to see if it was Alex.

I hesitantly stepped off the path and headed towards the big tree in the direction where I thought I saw him, breaking cobwebs as I went.

There were so many webs, and huge spiders that had spun them, that I had to wave my hands and arms in front of me as I went. It reminded me of all the crazy web-cracking karate moves I did when I walked the track for the first time years ago when I found the meadow. And here I was again. After breaking the first one, I did non-stop karate till I reached the big tree.

I half expected someone to step out from behind the tree as I approached. Half expected and dreaded it at the same time.

What if they stepped out and it wasn't Marvin or Alex? Or maybe they were long gone, whoever they were?

I stopped a couple of metres from the tree and said "Alex?" My own voice sounded out of place. I said it again. Still no answer.

I gingerly stepped around the tree, keeping a distance. I wasn't sure what I expected to find. Someone standing there? Someone with their back pressed up against the tree, hiding?

Or would they circle the tree in unison with me so that I'd never see them?

I had never expected, not in my worst nightmare, to see what I found.

It was hard to make out, but it was probably Alex. He was laid out on the ground. His body looked untouched, but his face, dear God, his face.

His expression looked like he was screaming when he died. His mouth was wide open but in the most hideous way. His jaw was broken so it no longer aligned with the top of his mouth, and it jutted out at a peculiar angle. But that wasn't the worst of it.

His eyes, or rather his lack of eyes, was the worst. His eyeballs were missing, like they had been ripped out. All that was left were ragged, bloody sockets.

I got such a fright when I saw those bloodied eye sockets, that I let out an involuntary sound that was a mixture of "Ahhh!" and "Ugh" and I stumbled backwards and fell. The shock of seeing him hit me so hard and so fast that it felt like someone had pushed me hard in the chest, knocking me over, rather than me just falling over on my own.

My backside hit some rocks as I went down, but I hardly noticed. I immediately got to my feet, staring at his face the whole time. I wanted to look away. I was desperate not to see it anymore, yet I was helpless and could only stare. And I kept on wondering, how could I have seen Alex duck behind the tree? No way could I have seen him moving a few seconds ago.

I backed away, back the way I'd come, no longer caring if I ran into cobwebs or not. After a few steps I turned and continued walking, looking back every 2 or 3 seconds to make sure that the body, with that awful face, wasn't following me.

Logic told me it couldn't, but I didn't care about logic anymore. I just wanted that thing to stay the hell away from me.

I made it back to the path again and turned to keep an eye on the big tree to make sure the body and face didn't rise from behind it.

The blood in the eye sockets was thick and mostly dry, so he hadn't only just died. It must have been hours ago, probably last night.

But I didn't care that he was long dead. I just wanted him to stay dead till I could get out of there.

I thought about calling the police, but that would mean staying there alone with Alex The Grim (why did I give him a nickname?) until they got there. No way, I told myself.

My hands were shaking and my whole body was doing jerky movements. It felt like I didn't have complete control over my limbs anymore.

I looked around for some large rocks. There were a few near me. I gathered them up and, while keeping an eye on the Alex Tree the whole time, placed them in a pile on the path opposite the tree to mark the spot, and ran.

I ran the whole way back to Forrest Lane. I didn't care if Alex The Grim was chasing me or not, I didn't want to look back or I'd break my pace and my priority was getting the hell out of the woods as fast as possible.

As soon as I was back on my own street, I stopped for a few seconds to catch my breath, and then I jogged to my front gate. Once I'd gone through and closed it, I felt safe. Safety must have been psychological because there's no way a waist high gate could protect me from a zombie that might be chasing me, but it still made me feel safer.

I went inside, still breathing heavily from my run. I took out the business card that Detective Simpson had given me when we first met. I rang him and told him what I'd found. He came straight over and arrived in less than 30 minutes, bringing several other police cars with him.

I'd thought that he'd want an explanation as to what I was doing in the woods, but he didn't.

He wanted me to take him straight to the body. I explained about the pile of rocks that would make it easy for him, but he was having none of it. He wanted me to show him exactly where I'd found the body.

It was getting dark, but I figured that going in with plenty of police protection would keep me safe. But then again, the pessimistic part of my brain reminded me that young Alex went missing while with the police. As I headed off into the woods with Detective Simpson and a small group of policemen with torches, I wished the pessimistic part of my brain would just shut up.

It was dark in amongst all the trees making it hard to see where my feet were stepping. It was a wonder that I'd managed to run all the way home earlier without tripping over all the roots and stones in the paths.

We eventually made it to my pile of rocks. I pointed out the big tree. Detective Simpson wanted me to walk with him to it, but I flatly refused. Not only did I not want to see the body again, or even part of it, I didn't want to go near it either. I didn't want to go with him and there was nothing he could do to make me.

Detective Simpson went ahead with two other policemen. I waited with the other four. We were all silent, waiting for the reaction of the others once they looked around the other side of the tree.

Their reaction was as I expected with lots of "Oh dear God!" and "What the hell happened here?" and vomiting and sounds of dry retching.

The three of them came back and walked me out of the woods, while the four that were waiting with me were sent to stay with the body.

I was still terrified and didn't want to be there. Someone had killed that boy and that someone could still be in here. And what if the police I was with got out of the woods, then realised I was no longer with them? They must have been thinking the same thing because they all kept glancing at me every few seconds. We were all nervous. We had all seen the body with its twisted grin and bloodied eye sockets. Walking through the dark woods wasn't the place to keep thinking about it, but we were all silently thinking about nothing else, and our pace was brisk, all of us clearly eager to get out of the woods. There were lots of sounds around us in the woods and tonight it all sounded eerie.

I thought that once we were safely out of the woods, my mind would calm down. But I was wrong. I couldn't get that image of the dead body out of my mind.

Outside the forensic teams arrived as well as more police, tracker dogs, all my neighbours, and Alex's father, Anthony.

As for me, I might have been out of the woods physically, but not psychologically. It was as though everything going on around me wasn't real anymore. It all seemed surreal.

The police wanted to know how I found the body. They kept suggesting that I'd heard Alex scream, which was understandable given the state of his face, and they kept asking if I'd seen any birds, particularly crows (apparently, they peck out fresh eyeballs.)

I did my best to explain that I'd seen someone go into the woods and I'd followed them to the big tree. I described the person I'd seen ducking behind the tree, and they agreed that it sounded like Alex, which was impossible because he'd been dead for hours. I said I thought so too, but the truth was the truth, and I couldn't change it. I was still shocked over what I'd seen and so at that moment I really couldn't care less if they believed me or not.

I also knew that the police were questioning my neighbours, and no doubt they were asking them about me and if they'd seen me going into the woods or behaving strangely. Poor Isabel was probably being questioned more than the others.

I sat on my front veranda, talking to the police on and off all night, and the whole time I couldn't get the image of Alex's contorted face out of my mind. It made me sick to think about it, yet I couldn't stop thinking about it. I felt numb and continued to answer question after question.

After a while it occurred to me that the police were asking the same questions in different ways. But there was nothing I could tell them because I didn't know anything.

At one point, I saw Isabel standing near my front gate, so I went down to talk to her. As we were standing there, over her shoulder I could just make out the shape of Marvin looking out one of his front windows. The house was dark, but I saw him.

As I looked at him, he stepped back from the window and blended into the darkness. Then the roller blind went down slowly, and it was as if he was never there. His actions made my flesh creep. I could literally feel my skin tense and untense all over my body in a wave. What was Marvin up to? What was he doing in the woods? I definitely saw him go in, but I never saw him come out. My mind had had enough horror tonight and Marvin was making it worse. No wonder my mind had defaulted to a dream-like state because accepting reality was too hard.

The rest of the night was long, and I continued to linger in my dreamlike state. We finally got rid of the police after they stopped questioning everyone, by 6 am, long after daylight.

I was so tired I didn't even bother going to bed. I simply flopped on the couch and fell asleep immediately.

I didn't wake up until 4pm. My mind was back in reality again. After a quick shower and change of clothes, I headed straight into town and to the pub. I didn't want to be alone. After yesterday I needed the company of people I knew and who trusted me, especially after the police had spent all night talking to me like I was a criminal.

I found a few guys there who I knew so I sat with them, ordered a pizza and a cold drink, and had a good talk with them.

I told them about finding Alex, although I left out the part about his face and missing eyeballs. They told me about all the latest gossip and who thinks whom had done what.

Interestingly, they all said that the police had been questioning everyone about the people in Forrest Lane, as though they thought we all might have had something to do with the murders.

Naturally none of the locals thought we were a bunch of child-murdering neighbours, but clearly the police did, or at least that was one possibility they were looking into.

But one thing we all agreed on, and so did the police and the media, that Mackarb had a macabre serial killer problem. And the parents of the remaining four teens were the most worried about it.

It was clear that someone, or someone's, were targeting their children, yet for some unfathomable reason, was only attacking them in the woods. So as long as they kept their children out of the woods, they were safe.

Or so they hoped.

# Ashes To Ashes

For the next few days, after Alex Newcomb was found dead in the woods, the police took to patrolling Forrest Lane constantly.

For weeks there'd only been two police officers and one patrol car at the top of the lane in front of the barrier they'd erected to keep everyone out except those who lived here. They were so strict about keeping people out, that no one who lived in the lane could get a delivery or have visitors without the police first knocking on their door and checking that it was all legitimate.

Now there were two police cars permanently parked at the top of the lane, and two extra police walking up and down all day and night.

The whole thing felt intrusive and annoying. Every time the patrolling police saw someone, they'd reach for their guns and keep their hands there until they recognised that it was only one of us. They also stood guard over every delivery truck or van, just in case.

When I spoke to my neighbours, it turned out they felt as annoyed with the patrolling as I was. We all felt that we had no privacy anymore and were being constantly watched.

Eventually we all agreed to speak to the patrolling duo and tell them to stop.

We all went out to talk to them at the same time. We told them that we didn't like being hounded like suspects.

The police assured us that they were only there to stop any more teens going into the woods.

"Oh, come on," said Trevor. "Do you really think that the parents of the remaining four boys would let them anywhere near the woods after everything that's happened?"

One of the police, a young female, said, "We thought that after the first murder, and the second, and the third. Do you see where I'm going with this?"

"Also," said the other officer, a man who looked like he was in his fifties, "We thought stopping them at the top of the lane would work. But we all know now that it didn't. If we weren't here and another boy is killed, you'd be asking us why we didn't do more, when clearly the barricades and the police presence only at the top of the lane wasn't enough to prevent another death."

None of us could argue with that logic.

He continued. "The boys came through several properties, jumping fences to get into the woods. That's why we're here checking all the properties all the time, so that they can't do that again.

Jane argued, "They came over the fence and through the garden of the empty house at the bottom of the street. It's unlikely that they'd come through one of our gardens."

"But it's possible." said the policeman.

Jack, who lived at the top of the lane opposite Isabel said, "It still makes us feel like criminals, putting your hands on your guns every time you see us."

"We're just always prepared. What if it's not you? What if it's a stranger, or worse, the killer? We're here to keep everyone safe."

He was right, but none of us wanted to admit it. I didn't say anything. I was still thinking about Jane saying, 'the empty house.' She thought the house was empty and no one corrected her. So, I was right. I was the only one who knew Marvin was there.

We weren't the only ones who were sick and tired of what was happening. All the locals hated having the police and reporters everywhere. It was bad enough dealing with the collective grief over the loss of four young boys, but there was also the fear of losing four more, and being dogged by police and reporters everywhere we went made it harder for everyone and made many people angry.

I knew how they felt. I just wanted all of it to go away, to get out of our town, and for everything to go back to normal. But I doubted there would ever be a 'normal' here ever again, or at least for many years. I wondered how many would move away once it was all over, or would these tragedies link us all emotionally for the rest of our lives?

They say that people who have experienced great trauma together, like a hijacking, a shooting, a bombing, or being held captive for a long time, share a strong emotional bond for the rest of their lives. Some say it's because only someone who went through it can understand how they feel and how it affected them. Others say it's because it made them care about each other while the tragedy was occurring because they were fearing for all their lives.

I wondered if perhaps the same thing would happen here in Mackarb once it was all over. At the time it didn't feel like it, especially with things like Mary accusing Frieda's son of having something to do with the murder of her son and punching her in the face. No emotional bonds there, although after Alex Newcomb was killed, Mary felt so bad about what she did, she went to the hospital to see Frieda and both women wept together over the loss of their sons. After that everyone seemed to calm down a bit, or at least lost some of their edginess.

Instead of blaming each other, they now feared strangers instead. Mackarb used to be like any other small town in the way the locals embraced visitors and were happy to chat and get to know them.

But not anymore. Now when they saw someone they didn't recognise, they'd look away, or watch them in a mistrusting way.

And there were many strangers coming to our little town, all with a morbid fascination of what was happening. Many didn't get to stay because there was nowhere to park their cars. Our car park in town is small and the streets around it are too narrow to park on, so there wasn't enough parking spaces for all the cars that had started to turn up every day.

Some visitors had started parking in the streets further out from the centre of town. Locals retaliated by getting up early and parking their own cars in the street and making sure they left nowhere for anyone else to park. There were whole streets of neighbours doing it. I guess that the common enemy is something else that draws people together, and at that time all strangers felt like enemies.

While everyone else's attention was on everything that was going on, my attention was drawn to Isabel. It was weird because I really liked her and I was sure she felt the same, but we hadn't yet found the time to move our relationship forward. We seemed to be at an impasse and any attempt at intimacy resulted in an interruption from the police or a neighbour.

So, on Saturday night, when Isabel invited me over for dinner, I made a 'move.' Not much of one, but at my age, starting an intimate relationship with a woman felt strangely awkward. Fifty years ago, I would have pulled her to me and kissed her passionately, while sliding my hand up under her shirt. I wouldn't have thought twice about it.

But now in my sixties, it all seemed somehow foreign, like it was something I just didn't do anymore. Whether it was because of my age or because it was so long since I'd been intimate with a woman, I wasn't sure. In fact, when I thought about it, it was years since I'd even THOUGHT about being intimate with a woman. Perhaps thinking about it too much now was my problem. As the Nike slogan says, 'Just do it.'

But do what? I'd forgotten the mating ritual and whether certain 'moves' were considered too fast or too slow. Or whether it's different when you're older. Who knew? As the saying goes, I don't know how to act my age because I've never been this old before.

But on Saturday night, there we were, sitting on her outdoor sofa on her front verandah, our half-drank glasses of wine sitting on the matching outdoor coffee table.

I stretched my arm up and out, bringing it down to rest around her shoulders, wondering how she'd react. It felt like a cheezy, teenage move. To my delight she leaned into me. I put my other hand under her chin and turned her face up to mine. She didn't resist.

We kissed, softly at first and then harder with more urgency. She turned her body towards me and put her hand on my thigh. I was wearing shorts that came down almost to my knees. Her hand was on the flesh above my knee and slid up my shorts. I groaned excitedly.

I slid my hand down from under her chin, over the outside of her blouse, to her breast. I felt her body stiffen under my touch and she moaned in pleasure.

Any doubts I might have had about her not wanting to be intimate with me melted away in that moment.

Isabel pulled away from me, picked up her glass of wine and said, "Let's finish these inside."

I picked up my glass, she took my hand and led me inside, locking the door behind us.

*	*	*

The next night, Sunday, I sat on my front verandah late in the evening, sipping a cup of tea. I felt good. I hadn't felt this good in a long time.

I'd stayed with Isabel till late the night before. She wanted me to stay the night but understood when I said that too many people would see me leaving the next morning (I could just imagine all the police waving to me as I stepped off her front porch, saying, "Morning. Did you enjoy her last night?)

No. It was better if no one knew about us because it was no one else's business and I wanted to keep it that way. Isabel agreed.

I snuck out while the patrols were up the top of the lane talking to the barricade cops. So much for them guarding the lane and not missing anyone. But it was to my advantage, so I didn't complain.

Before I left, I invited Isabel round for breakfast. I wanted to see her again as soon as I could.

When she arrived the next morning, we hugged and kissed, enjoying our new closeness.

We ate breakfast inside away from prying eyes and held hands across the table while we finished our coffee. I poured us each a second cup which we took out and drank on the back verandah.

We held hands and chatted like teenagers and laughed a lot. It felt so good to be with her.

We enjoyed talking so much that I went in and made us another cup of coffee each. It felt silly, but I never wanted the morning to end. But of course, it eventually did.

After Isabel left, I washed the dishes and thought to myself, "Wow. I've got a girlfriend," and then smiled at my own childishness. But it was true, Isabel and I were a couple and had arranged to meet up the next day too because that's what couples do. They make plans together.

While I sat and sipped my tea (herbal, of course, chamomile to be exact) I read through some of my crazy fan mail. From the things they wrote I figured there were a lot of crazy women around. One of them wrote that she was currently looking to buy a house in Mackarb and wanted me to come over for dinner when she moved in. I hoped she was kidding about moving here, or I'd never get rid of her.

Another woman said I was her husband in a previous life, and she'd recognised me straight away. She even talked about places we'd been and children we'd had, and other things, none of which I had any idea about. What a weirdo, and the rest of the fan mail I got told me she was far from being the only crazy old lady.

Movement out in the street caught my eye. I wasn't sure why I looked up because I was used to having two police walking up and down all the time, so I mostly didn't bother looking if there was someone walking in the lane.

But it wasn't the police. It was someone walking as though they were in a trance, the way zombies walk in bad horror movies, staring straight ahead, barely lifting their feet off the ground, arms hanging limply by their sides.

Where were the police? No doubt chatting at the top of the road like they were the night before when I left Isabel's. The person was halfway down the lane, somewhat silhouetted because the only streetlight was behind them. They were walking down the middle of the road.

As they approached, I literally felt my stomach sink. It was one of The Octo Gang. I wondered how the hell he'd gotten past the police. How did they not see him?

By the time he passed my gate I could see who it was. Tracey Nolan, son of Elspeth and Craig Nolan. I had to do something. I couldn't just let him walk into the woods alone.

"Tracey!" I called out, but he just kept up his zombie walk, not reacting at all to my voice.

I called louder. "Tracey!" He was at the entrance to the woods by then and he walked around the caution tape and melted into the darkness out of sight, never breaking his stride.

I sat there not knowing what to do. There was no way I was going to go into the woods. But there had clearly been something wrong with him. My mind was racing with all the thoughts about what I should do. Maybe I should scream for the police to get down here and ask them how the hell Tracey had made it all the way down the lane and into the woods without them seeing him.

I stood up. The easiest and quickest thing would be to go up to the police and tell them to go get the kid out of there. I walked to my gate and suddenly stopped. I started to tremble. I was unable to move, too afraid to reach out and open the gate.

It was Marvin, walking out of the woods. He stopped and even though he hadn't looked my way at all while he was walking, he seemed to know I was there. He turned to look at me, then quickly dashed down the side of his house, and disappeared into the darkness.

My heart thumped and my body shook. What had he done to the boy? Was it Marvin who'd put the kid in a trance-like state?

I stared at Marvin's house, waiting for a light to go on, but as usual the place remained dark.

Surely he hadn't hurt the boy. There hadn't even been time to do anything. It doesn't take long to stab someone; my logical mind told me.

But I didn't have time to think about it. I had to get help. When I put out my hand to open the gate, I saw how much I was trembling. My hand was shaking and I couldn't stop it. It was shaking so much that I struggled to open the simple latch.

I ran up the lane, not daring to look at Marvin's house. If he was watching out the window, I didn't want to know.

The lane was only a slight incline, but I was breathing heavily by the time I was halfway up. I laboured on till I was about three quarters there. I could see all four police chatting in a group as usual. I wanted to call out to them, but I was too out of breath. I bent over, hands on thighs, panting hard.

They must have seen me, or heard me breathing, because two of the police came down to me.

"What are you doing? Are you okay?"

I looked up to see an older policeman and a young policewoman, both of whom I'd seen before. It was the policeman who'd spoken.

I took a few more heavy breaths. "Why didn't you stop him?"

They exchanged a puzzled look.

"The teenage boy, Tracey Nolan," I panted.

"What about him?" asked the young policewoman.

"He went into the woods."

"What? When?" She asked.

"Just now. That's what I ran up here to tell you."

"Where did he come from?"

"He was walking down the street."

"No way," she argued. "He couldn't have come past us."

"And yet he did." I was instantly angry.

"You're supposed to be walking up and down the lane, so this ones on you."

The male police officer bristled, clearly annoyed at being told he wasn't doing his job, even if I didn't actually say it. But it was their fault that the teenager had gone into the woods because they weren't where they were supposed to be, and it wasn't the first time. Last night they were all huddled at the top of the lane when I left Isabel's place, and they were huddled there again tonight.

"We had only stopped to talk to our colleagues for a few seconds. We'd only just stopped patrolling."

I put my hand up to stop him talking. How dare he lie to me. "Bullshit. You were up there while the boy walked down the street and you were there the whole time I was running up here, so don't lie to me." Now that I was on a roll it was hard to stop. "You were given one job; protect the teenagers. Yet another one has disappeared in the woods. I ran up here to tell you, and all you do is tell me how wrong I am about what happened.

"Not only that, but instead of going straight in there to find him, you stand here and make out like it's all about you. YOU didn't do anything wrong. Well, I'm going home now to call the boy's parents and tell them how their son is missing but not to worry because it's not the police's fault, even though their only job was to keep him safe. AND I'll tell them that when I told you he was alone in the woods, you did nothing."

I turned and stomped back home. I was furious. I ran up to tell them another teenager was in the woods and they all but called me a liar and didn't even rush down to find him. I'd always had respect for the police, but right then I didn't.

"Harold!" It was a voice I was glad to hear. I stopped and turned around. Isabel was running to catch up with me. "What's going on? You sounded angry just then." As she spoke, the barriers were pulled aside and the two police cars came rushing down the street, their red and blue lights flashing, which I guessed was for our benefit because there was no one else around.

We continued walking back to my place. Seeing her had instantly improved my mood, but I was still annoyed with the police. "I just had the most frustrating conversation with them. I ran up to talk to them and it went like this; There's another teenager gone into the woods. It's not our fault."

Isabel was stunned. "There's another one in the woods?"

"Yep. He came walking straight down the lane with no police anywhere to stop him."

"Who was it?"

"Tracey Nolan. I called out to him, but he ignored me and carried on straight into the woods without stopping. Anyway, it's late, were you still up?"

"Yeah, I was doing some sewing and I wanted to finish it before I went to bed. I was watching a movie at the same time. I was putting everything away and I turned off the TV when I heard your raised voice loud and clear through the open windows. Did they really say it wasn't their fault?"

"Yeah. Didn't rush off to go look for him. First, they said there was no way anyone could have got past them, then they made an excuse as to why they didn't see him."

"Were they all gas bagging at the top of the lane again?"

"I reckon it's what they do every night when they think no one's looking."

We'd reached my house. "Tea?" I asked."

"Love one," she said.

We sat on the sofa swing on the front veranda to drink our tea and watch what was going on. More police arrived, police dogs too. They quickly set up big lights and went to search the woods.

Isabel and I finished our tea. I was tired and didn't really want to stay up any longer. I felt bad because there was a teenager missing, probably murdered, and all I wanted to do was go to sleep. I knew that if we sat there much longer, the police would want to interview us.

As if reading my mind Isabel said, "I don't want to seem heartless, but I'm tired and if we stay here much longer we'll be interviewed."

"I was just thinking the same thing and there's nothing we can tell them anyway."

"I think we both know how this is going to end."

"Sadly, yes."

Isabel leaned over, gave me a kiss then gave me her empty cup. "Night."

"Good night." I said. Before she'd even walked to the road I'd gone inside and shut my door on the world, grateful that my bedroom was at the back of the house.

I slept soundly that night which made me feel a bit guilty, knowing that people I knew had most likely lost their son last night and I literally did not lose a wink of sleep over it. But then again, whether I slept well or not wouldn't change what was happening to them.

During the night I heard someone knocking at my door. I figured it must be the police and I didn't want to talk to them because I was tired, I had nothing to tell them, and because I was still annoyed with them. So, I turned over and went straight back to sleep.

I'd only been up an hour the next morning when they knocked again. It was my usual Detective John Simpson and his young sidekick, Peter Norman. I went out and sat at the table on the verandah with them.

As usual it was Detective Simpson who did most of the talking.

"So, Harold, I hear that it was you who saw young Tracey Nolan going into the woods last night."

I didn't respond.

"Well, was it?"

"I hadn't realised it was a question, but yes, it was me."

"What time was that?"

"Just before I told those clowns at the top of the street that I'd seen him. Not that they believed me. Did they tell you? They stood there calling me a liar and saying that no one could have walked down the street without them seeing something and then making up some lame bullshit excuse about how it wasn't their fault."

Detective Simpson exchanged a glance at his partner and said, "I'd heard that you'd accused them of not doing their job, but if the boy had entered the lane through someone's property again, they may have missed him."

I cut in. "Missed him? Last night AND the night before, all four of them were stood chatting and laughing at the top of the lane. Two of them are supposed to be patrolling up and down at all times."

"They said they'd just stopped to talk to their colleagues for a few seconds which isn't unreasonable."

"A few seconds? What do you call a few seconds?" I was even more annoyed now that he was defending them when he wasn't even there.

"Probably less than a minute."

"Then riddle me this, Batman. How did I see them at the top of the lane when I came outside with a cup of tea, drink half my tea, read two letters, see the boy walk past my neighbour's house, call to him twice as he walked into the woods, and then get up and run to nearly the top of the lane, all in less than one minute?"

The two detectives just stared at me for a few seconds then the younger one said, "Maybe it was more than a minute."

They had to be kidding me. "You two weren't even there so you don't know what happened. The four of them were also stood there the previous night when I left a neighbour's house and walked down to mine without being seen. I'm not stupid."

"Look," said Detective Simpson. "Let's put this aside for now. The reason we're asking is because the timeline doesn't fit."

"What timeline?"

"The boy's death."

"So, he is dead?"

"Didn't anyone tell you?"

"No. I went to bed last night and hadn't been up long before you got here. I haven't seen the news either. What happened to him?"

"It took a long time to find him last night because he'd been buried. Alive."

"Buried? What do you mean, buried?"

"He was found in a deep grave. We couldn't find him. But the cadaver dogs did. They found the body in a part of the woods that we'd already searched, so how was it that he was buried so quickly? That's why I need to know what time you saw the boy."

"My answer isn't going to change, even with this new information. I saw him walk down the lane and I ran to tell the police."

"How was he walking? Was he walking fast, running, was he looking around?"

I hesitated briefly, wondering just how much detail to give them. "He was walking slowly, staring straight ahead. I called to him a couple of times. But he didn't respond. He just kept walking and staring."

"Was there anyone with him?"

"No, I would have told you if there was. How do you know he was alive when he was buried?"

"The forensic team at the scene said he'd inhaled dirt."

"Oh God. I don't think I wanted to know that. Are you saying that someone had already dug a grave then lured him into the woods to throw him in and bury him?"

"That's what it looks like. And with no other noticeable injuries it looks like he laid on his back and allowed someone to throw dirt all over him."

I was silent. It was hard to take in what they were saying. My mind struggled to cope with believing it was real.

Detective Simpson added, "Unless the toxicity test comes back showing something different. It's possible that someone drugged him. But we won't know until after the autopsy."

Hearing that didn't make it any better. "I don't know what to tell you. I saw Tracey Nolan walk quietly and determinedly into the woods. I ran up the street immediately to report it. The end."

But I didn't tell them that Tracey had been walking in a trance-like state because I thought it would sound crazy. I also hadn't told them about Marvin because that would sound crazy too. No one had seen Marvin. No one knew of his existence but me. And anyway, telling them that I'd seen Marvin come out of the woods and walk around the back of his house wouldn't make any difference because he came out a few seconds after Tracey went in. He hadn't had time to bury someone. Or had he? Could Marvin even do that?

A boy had disappeared in the woods, I saw Marvin, then reported the missing boy to the police, and somehow, during that small window of time, he was buried alive in the woods.

Once again, it all came back to Marvin.

Or did it?

I had to wonder if maybe, just maybe, I was so obsessed with convincing myself that Marvin had something to do with all the murders, that no matter what he did, it looked suspicious to me.

But there was no denying that he always seemed to be around when someone died.

# Suffocated

I woke up the next morning feeling tired after spending the night restlessly. I must have woken up a dozen times. It had also been a hot and humid night which hadn't helped.

All night I couldn't stop thinking about the awful way that poor, young Tracey Nolan had died. Who would do such a thing? Who would even THINK of doing such a thing?

'What are you doing tonight?'

'Oh, I'm just going to go and bury someone alive. See you later.'

Did Marvin have something to do with it? I wasn't sure. The man was somewhat of an enigma. Yet he always seemed to be somehow in the middle of all the creepy stuff going on in our town, while at the same time he seemed to be doing nothing at all. Maybe I was just getting old and paranoid.

I turned onto my back, yawned, stretched, then threw back the covers and got out of bed. After I'd showered and dressed, I looked out the front window and saw that there was still police and other official-looking people out in the lane, so I decided to stay indoors and pretend I wasn't there.

After lunch I heard familiar voices outside. I went out and saw all my neighbours, including Isabel, standing in the middle of the road halfway up the street, talking. I went to join them. They turned as I approached them.

"Isabel was just telling us about what happened," said Trevor.

"It's disgusting that young Tracey got into the woods with the police here to stop it," I said. "It shouldn't have happened."

Sharon looked around at all the other people in the lane and said, "Come on. Let's go to our place and talk privately."

She and Bruce led us all round the side of their house which is next to mine, and onto their back patio where they have an eight-seater table in the middle.

We all sat down, and Sharon went inside and brought out cold drinks for everyone.

Bruce said, "We've been talking to many locals today. The murders are all anyone can talk about."

Isabel said, "Well it's not surprising. This is like the kind of thing that happens in horror movies not in real life, and not in our quiet little street."

Sharon said to Isabel, "It's our little street that they're all talking about now."

I said, "Why? Well, apart from the obvious."

Janet leaned forward and said, "They're suspicious of all of us who live in Forrest Lane."

"What?" The rest of us said in unison.

"Do they think we're all murderers?" asked Isabel.

"No," said Jane. "But they think we all know more than we're telling."

"What?" I said. "How can we know more than anyone else?"

"Think about it," said Jack. "It all happens in the woods, but it all starts in the lane. We all keep saying we see the kids go in there but swear we see no one else."

Everyone started talking at once, throwing their hands in the air and sitting back in their seats indignantly. No one could believe that others thought we were helping a murderer to kill local kids.

But Jack and Doreen, and Jane and Trevor, all told us that the locals had even pointed out that no one in Forrest Lane had any children, a mundane fact, yet now it cast more suspicion on us. Apparently, the locals were also suggesting that we all must hear what goes on in the woods, especially me because I live right next to it. They said that some had even asked if I had a door in my back fence directly into the woods. It seemed like fear was making people crazy.

Isabel said, "The worst part isn't what's already happened, or how people are turning on each other, it's the waiting, knowing that something is coming next, but we don't know when." No one disagreed. But we all did agree that this waiting must be worse for the families of the remaining three teenagers.

The next day, Tuesday, the police were back at my place asking to speak with me again. It was my usual two detectives. I sat with them at the table on the front veranda. It was another hot day, so I brought out three cold glasses of ginger beer.

"I really don't know what else I can tell you," I said to them.

The lane was now empty of police and others, except for the two officers who were walking up and down all the time.

Detective Simpson said, "It's not just you. We're talking to everyone in Forrest Lane because maybe, just maybe, there's something you've seen but didn't think it was important to mention. Or maybe there's something you've forgotten, so if we go over it all one more time we'll see if anything new comes up."

I sighed in frustration. "That will take hours. There's been five murders."

"Yes, and there might be three more if we don't do something to stop it."

"So, you don't have any clue who's doing it?"

Detective Simpson took a long swallow of his drink as though giving himself time to think of an answer. He put down his glass and said slowly, "The short answer is no."

"Do you have any suspects? I can't imagine it being anyone local."

"Why not? Who else would have a reason for wanting the kids dead?"

He was right. Why would anyone do it? "So, there's no clues? What do they call it, crime scene evidence?"

"That would have been handy, but no. Not a thing. Each murder that happens creates more questions than answers. The first kid was scared to death. But scared of what? The last kid was buried alive, but why did he go in there alone? Are you sure you didn't see anyone else in the lane that night?"

I sat back, exasperated. "There were four police at the top of the lane that night. If they didn't see anyone, how could I?"

"You were closest to the boy," said Detective Simpson.

"It was late. It was dark. He was walking alone." I felt the usual pang of guilt for not mentioning Marvin. But maybe I could give them a hint, so I said, "What about the empty house across the road? Have you checked there isn't a crazed murderer hiding in there?"

"Naturally that was one of the first places we checked. Once we obtained a key, we observed that the house has been empty for some time."

His answer surprised me. I had no idea they'd been in there. "No one at all? How could you tell?"

"I didn't go in there personally, but the officers who did said there was no evidence of anyone living or hiding there."

"When was this?"

"Oh, I don't know. Probably after the first boy was found. Why"

"I just didn't see anyone go in there."

"Let me know if you do," he said, half-jokingly.

After that we briefly went over what I'd seen and heard when each incident happened, but I had nothing new to add and I was annoyed because I thought they were wasting everyone's time. None of us had seen anything. Nothing at all.

The police were acting just like the locals, thinking that everyone in Forrest Lane knew more than they were telling.

After they left, I went into town to do some shopping. I ran into Isabel. We briefly discussed being interviewed by the police again and how annoying it was. It seemed they'd spoken to her the day before. I invited her to dinner so we could talk more.

At the supermarket I bought salad, pasta, and garlic bread, and then went to the bottle shop to get a bottle of wine to go with it. I already had several bottles at home, but I wanted to buy one specifically for our dinner date simply because it somehow seemed appropriate.

I walked home in high spirits, excited to spend time alone with Isabel again. It did feel kind of silly being so happy about a date. I hadn't felt like this since I first met my wife. We were crazy about each other right from the start. We seemed to be such a good fit for each other. It also felt a bit like that with Isabel. She was the first woman I'd had an intimate relationship with since Maggie died. And as soon as I saw her, I knew there was something about her, but I was damned if I knew what it was. I just wanted to get to know her and after our one, glorious, intimate night together, I knew she felt the same.

But our attempt at having a relationship was somewhat always disrupted and disturbed by all the killings, so it was a wonder we ever managed to get together at all. But we did, even though it was a bizarre way to start a relationship, surrounded by police, forensic teams, dead bodies, and reporters.

I suddenly stopped walking because there in front of me was Susan Jackson and her ever-present cameraman. "Harold," she smiled. "I'm so glad to see you again. Can we do an interview?"

I was amused that she and I had now become 'we.' I hadn't seen her for a while, so I said, "Sure." My mood was high, so I wasn't too bothered about talking to her.

She turned to her cameraman and said, "Roll." Then she adjusted and straightened her jacket, turned to face me, and said. "Harold, you live in Forrest Lane right next to the entrance to the woods and you've been in constant communication with the police. In fact, I understand that it was you who discovered one of the bodies."

She pointed her microphone at me, and her cameraman turned his camera to me. "Well Susan, I firstly want to say thank you for announcing exactly where I live on national television." Her smile instantly disappeared, and I could see the realisation of what she'd said spreading across her face. But I was just joking with her. Everyone in the whole country must know I live on Forrest Lane because she'd filmed me right outside my house several times.

I carried on quickly. "Sadly, yes. I did find one of the kids in the woods."

She recovered her smile instantly. "What were you doing in there?"

"Just walking. I'd gone quite a way when I saw him."

"Do many people still go into the woods?"

"Not from our street."

"Do the police have any idea about who's committing these terrible crimes, or why?"

"Not to my knowledge, but I don't know everything the police do or what they know."

"What about the people here in town? How are they coping with what's going on?"

"Naturally they're all devastated, and afraid, especially the parents of the other teenagers. But what's hardest to cope with is all the reporters asking questions all the time." I smiled as I said the last sentence.

Susan smiled back and said, "Oh touché Harold." She turned to face the camera and said, "As you can see, the mood is still somber, but the locals have not lost their sense of humour. This is Susan Jackson reporting from Mackarb." She gave a bright smile to the camera then made a throat cutting gesture with her hand. The cameraman turned off the camera and lowered it to the ground.

"See ya," I said and carried on walking.

I made dinner and showered later, still looking forward to seeing Isabel again. I just hoped we could have a normal conversation for a change, but of course I knew we wouldn't, not with everything that was happening.

We ate inside and sat outside on the sofa swing as usual with our second glass of wine.

Sitting there while the sun went down should have been a romantic setting, but it was spoiled by the constant presence of two police constantly walking up and down the street. I'd also had to light a couple of mosquito coils and put them at either side of us to keep the mosquitoes away. That was the problem with the warm humid weather we'd been having was that it brought all the insects out, especially the ones that bite, and mosquito coils don't smell the nicest. Not romantic at all, but we had no choice.

When we'd finished our wine, I went inside to pour us each a third glass and when I came back out the two officers were standing on the veranda talking to Isabel.

"It's getting harder," the slim, younger one was saying.

"What is?" I asked as I sat down next to Isabel and handed her one of the wine glasses.

"Keeping people out of the woods," he said. "We've stopped them all getting in here, which is the easiest way in, but they keep finding a way in through other places. We try and keep then out at the obvious entrances, but there's no way we can stop them altogether."

"What are they doing in there?" asked Isabel.

The older, stocky officer answered. "They're a bunch of looky-loos, hoping to see something grisly.

The younger man said, "A few days ago we stopped a group of ghost hunters. They had professional video equipment and everything, so it looked like they were planning to make a documentary or a movie or something."

Isabel shook her head. "It doesn't surprise me. People here are grieving and scared, yet all other people want to do is gawp and use it as cheap entertainment. I bet there's already people writing books and making movies about it. The TV crime shows will have content for their shows for years."

The older officer nodded at me and said, "If they do make TV shows and movies about this, I bet you'll be in it. I keep seeing you on the news all the time."

I laughed. "I know. I get lots of crazy fan mail too. You know, women actually write letters to me."

"Really? What about?"

"Their letters range from they like seeing me to they want to marry me."

Isabel looked at me. "Really? They want to marry you?"

I laughed again. "Yep. There's a whole bunch of crazy old ladies out there. They seem to want to mother me too. Some want to come and stay with me here, and straight away."

Isabel grimaced. "Yeesh!"

The younger policeman laughed and said to Isabel, "He's not kidding. We've had a few of them already at the top of the street trying to get through. They even have their suitcases with them."

"You're joking," I said, half laughing, half horrified.

"Nope. People are either trying get to the woods or trying to get to you."

I was speechless for several seconds. I put my palm up to him. "Just stop. Things are already scary enough around here."

I wished the police would go away so that Isabel and I could be alone. Unfortunately, they seemed to have nothing else to do. So, we ended up talking to them for a while longer, but we did learn that the police had absolutely no idea who was doing all the killings. Which was worrying.

When they finally went, I made herbal tea for Isabel and I. We'd already finished the bottle of wine and it seemed dangerous to open another one in case we finished that one too.

We sat outside on the sofa swing. I put my hand on Isabel's thigh, on the soft material of her long skirt. She reciprocated by putting her hand on my thigh, on the thin cotton of my knee-length shorts.

I turned to kiss her when there was a sudden loud thud from inside the woods. We both jolted and looked towards the trees at the end of the lane. I felt Isabel tense up, and no doubt she felt me tense up as well. I was scared.

"What was that?" she whispered. "Do you think there's somebody in there?"

"Normally I'd say no, but now I'm not so sure." We both continued to stare into the darkness. There was a sudden loud snap, followed by a rustling sound.

Isabel's grip tightened on my thigh. "It could be an animal," she said, unconvincingly.

I had no intention of being her protector. Cowardice was my default setting in situations like this, especially if I was with someone who would expect me to protect them too. "Usually, I'd just shrug and say yeah, it probably is an animal. But now it's no longer wise to make these assumptions. Let's continue this party inside away from unknowns in the woods, and chatty policemen who might return."

"I agree. We need not take a chance with either," she said as we both stood up. We swiftly moved inside and locked the door. I felt a twinge of annoyance that the woods that had been so pleasant to sit by at night, were now a place to be feared. And it was probably just one person who'd ruined it for everyone.

But tonight, it worked out for the best. Whatever we'd heard came to nothing and moving inside to the couch with Isabel progressed to another intimate night together.

For the next few days nothing bad happened in the woods, but it did nothing to quell the fear and the feelings of unease.

I went into town a couple of times, once to get more groceries, and once to have a drink at the pub. Both times I was besieged by reporters. I was still a fan favourite with the viewers it seemed, and I was still getting mail from the crazy ones.

The only reporter I talked to now was Susan Jackson. They all wanted to talk to me and tried to stop me everywhere I went. Even when I was at the pub, they were filming me through the windows, which I didn't know about until I saw it on TV.

So, I chose Susan because I already knew her from speaking with her the whole way through.

But this particular day I still had nothing to tell her about what was happening, but she seemed more interested in emotional stories about how everyone was feeling.

She caught up with me at the pub, which was not unusual seeing as all the media people were staying there. I was sitting with Stephen and his wife, Nancy, and Isabel, when she approached.

She walked up to our table, camera man in tow as usual, and said, "Hey Harold. I'm glad I caught you here with your friends. It would be great to do an interview with you all, just to get a general feel of how things are affecting everyone here."

The other three all looked at me. "It's fine with me," I said, assuming that their silence meant acceptance.

"Great," said Susan, also assuming that everyone had already agreed on my say so.

She asked the others what their names were and made a note in a small notebook that she pulled out of her jacket pocket. I'd expected her to pull out her phone and tap their names in. "So, you're not high-tech then," I said, nodding at her notebook.

"God no. It's so much easier and quicker to make notes by hand instead of scrolling through them all on my phone." I didn't blame her. I felt the same way.

Once she'd written down everyone's names, making sure to get the correct spelling and questioning Isabel because she had the same surname as me, she put her notebook and pen back in her pocket, arranged herself and her camera man to get the right angle, and said, "Roll." The camera man obliged. To the camera she said, "I'm here at Mackarbee Hotel here in Mackarb, with some of the locals, Stephen and Nancy Boulder, Isabel Johnson, and a now familiar face, Harold Johnson, who, by the way, is not related to Isabel. They both assure me that even though they live in the same street and share the same last name, it's just a coincidence."

She turned to the four of us. "So, Stephen, how is the general feeling in town these days?" How is everyone coping?"

Stephen looked surprised that she'd singled him out first, but he quickly recovered. "As you can imagine, the mood here can be pretty sombre. It's a terrible time for the parents and families of the boys who've been murdered, and a worry for all the other parents as well."

Susan moved the microphone to Stephen's wife. "What about you, Nancy? Is it different now in Mackarb?"

Nancy blushed. "Well, it's certainly not the relaxed and happy place it used to be, and it's not helped by all the strangers coming here and the police trying to keep them away."

"Isabel?" she said, pointing the microphone at her. Isabel said, "Living in Forrest Lane has been particularly difficult for us all, but that doesn't even begin to compare to the families who've lost their boys."

"And Harold?"

"Our town will never be the same. Never. But right now, the hardest thing is waiting for whatever is going to come next. We all know that there's probably more to come so no one can relax, and no one can stop what's happening. Not even the police."

"Are you saying that the police aren't doing their job?"

"Not at all. Everything that's happened here seems so bizarre and how it's all happening seems impossible, yet it happens, right here under everyone's proverbial noses. And maybe if the police weren't so busy keeping people out of the woods, the ones who just come to gawp at our tragedy, then they could put all their effort into preventing more murders." I looked directly into the camera and said, "So stay away people!"

"Well said, Harold." Susan turned back to the camera. "You heard it. The police are dealing with multiple murders and their work is being hampered because people keep besieging this small town for nothing more than cheap entertainment. So please, everyone, stay away and let the police do their job.

"This is Susan Jackson in Mackarb." She made her usual 'cut' motion with her finger across her throat, and said, "Thanks so much guys," and left, with her camera man following obediently behind as usual.

Somehow, being interviewed had killed the mood. We sat and talked for a while till we'd finished our drinks, then we all went home.

Once again, for the next few days, nothing bad happened in Mackarb, so people relaxed slightly. It always amazed me how quickly people start to let go. Perhaps it was hope that it was all over, because all we had was hope. Or maybe it was because we were all so emotionally wound that we needed to loosen up whenever we could.

Whatever the reason, the reprieve was only the calm before the storm.

# Stormy Weather

It was late Sunday afternoon. I was sitting on my front veranda thinking about everything that had happened and how upset and nervous everyone was. It was a terrible time for our little town, and I wished it would all just stop and go away, even though I knew that it never would. Even if nothing else happened, our town, and its people, would never be the same again.

The only positive thing that had happened, if you can call it positive, is that house prices here had more than doubled. According to the real estate offices, people were making ridiculous offers on houses here, whether they were for sale or not. Yet, ironically, no one wanted to sell anymore. House sales in Mackarb had stopped for the time being.

I was sitting and enjoying a cup of coffee when, out of the corner of my eye, I saw movement across the road. I looked up and saw Marvin walking into the woods. I froze as I watched him disappear out of sight amongst the trees. If it had been anyone else it wouldn't have bothered me. But anything about Marvin was worrying.

I looked up the road to see if anyone one else was around. Was I still the only one who had ever seen him? The two patrolling police officers were almost at the top of the lane, backs towards the woods, chatting happily. They turned slowly as they neared the barrier and began to walk back down. Marvin must have timed his exit to make sure he wasn't seen. He hadn't noticed me watching him, but from experience I knew that it didn't necessarily mean he hadn't seen me. More than once he'd turned to look at me as though he felt me sitting here rather than saw me.

I'd nearly finished my coffee and was just thinking about going inside when I'd seen Marvin. It piqued my curiosity. I had to know what he was doing and how long he was going to be in the woods. I decided to sit there as long as I had to. It turned out I had to sit there for almost an hour before Marvin returned. As soon as I saw him I looked up the street. The two police were once again nearly at the top of the lane, their backs to the woods.

Marvin looked the same as when he went in. His clothes weren't dirty or untidy and he wasn't sweating despite it being a really warm day. For all intents and purposes it looked like he'd just gone for a walk. But I didn't believe that. Marvin was looking down and didn't see me. He walked along the side of his house and disappeared out of sight.

I looked at the woods, wondering what would happen next. I wanted to look away, but it must be the same phenomena that happens when people see a car crash. They want to look away but can't. I stared at the entrance to the woods for quite a while. I saw the two police walk down the lane and back up several times. Eventually I gave up and went inside to have dinner and a shower.

Later, I came back outside and sat at the table on the veranda, in the dark, waiting and watching. I had no idea what I was waiting for, but I just had a strong feeling after seeing Marvin that something was about to happen, and it wasn't going to be something good.

I sat there for over an hour, watching the police walk up and down several times, until I heard it. Noises in the woods, soft noises. I couldn't make out what they were, but it sounded like some kind of movement. I was instantly nervous. After a few seconds, another sound began. It sounded like whispering, chanting almost. It was so soft I wondered if I was actually hearing it or if it was my fearful mind imagining it. I was scared. Damn scared. I wanted to get up and bolt inside, but I had to know what the quiet noises were, whether or not they were real or just my overactive imagination.

Where were the damn police when you needed them? I looked up the lane. The two policemen were leaning on the barrier at the top of the street, chatting to the other two officers, all out of earshot of the creepy sounds from the woods. The whispering continued. It became slightly louder and then I knew I wasn't imagining it. I fled inside and locked the door.

From the safety of the inside of my house, I went to the side window and pulled back the curtain just an inch and peered out into the darkness. I couldn't see anything. I could barely make out the entrance to the woods at all. I moved my face closer to the window until my eyes were nearly touching the glass. I squinted to try to see better. In the dark, I could just about make out the fence and the barrier to the woods.

Suddenly a face appeared at the other side of the glass. It was as close to the outside as I was to the inside. I flung myself backwards, almost tearing the curtain off the rail as I went. A strange little scream escaped my throat.

My heart was hammering in my chest. I let go of the curtain, grateful as it flapped back into place, obscuring the window and anyone who might be looking through it. I stood there panting. Had there really been someone out there looking back at me? Or did I just see the reflection of my own face? Either way it scared the hell out of me. I kept repeating to myself that it was just my own reflection. But I didn't believe it.

I calmed my panting and tried to listen to see if I could hear anything outside, like running footsteps. But there was nothing. I hadn't heard anything before I saw the face at the window and there was nothing to hear now. That made it worse to think that someone had snuck up through my garden and left again without making a sound. Standing there in that moment, I was more frightened than I'd ever been in my whole life. My heart was beating hard in my chest, and I was too afraid to move. But I had to do something.

I walked towards the window, intending to pull back the curtain and see if there was anyone out there. But as soon as my hand touched the fabric, I knew I couldn't do it. What would happen if the face was still outside the window? What would happen if it wasn't there? Would it make me feel any better if it was gone? I realised that I didn't really want to see if the face was there or not, because one would make me feel worse, and the other wouldn't reassure me at all. And, on reflection (no pun intended), I didn't believe it was my own face that I saw because it appeared AFTER I looked outside. If it was my own reflection, it would have already been there.

I figured that eventually the police would walk down the street and if there was anyone around, they would scare them off. But why would there be someone outside in my garden in the first place? I had no idea, but then again, nothing about what was happening made any sense.

To calm myself down, I grabbed a beer out of the fridge and sat down and watched TV for a couple of hours, during which time I had a second beer too, and I muted the sound every now and again to see if I could hear anything from outside. But there was nothing. Watching TV did help to get my mind off what had just happened and into a TV show instead. Then I went nervously to bed and tossed and turned until I finally drifted to sleep.

The next morning (Monday) I woke to the police knocking at my door. I knew it was the police because no one knocks as loud and insistently as they do. It was only 6.30.

I went to the toilet, stretched, and went to answer the door. They knocked the whole time. Unsurprisingly it was Detectives Simpson and Norman. "So, you've still not solved it yet?" I asked them.

"Good morning Harold. We need to talk to you."

"Yeah, well I was in bed, so you'll have to wait. I need to get dressed." I shut the door, put the kettle on, got dressed, made my bed, made myself a cup of coffee and took it outside with me. The two detectives were sitting at the table. I sat down with them.

For a change, Detective Peter Norman spoke first. "Have you heard what happened last night?"

"I told you. I was in bed."

"The remaining three boys have gone missing." Three at once? I was surprised but tried not to show it. I just didn't feel like talking to them because I never had anything to tell them.

"What's that got to do with me?"

"You live closest to the woods."

"What makes you think that's where they are?"

"It's the obvious place."

"Have you looked?"

"Yes. Not thoroughly, but we have done a preliminary search."

Detective Simpson broke in. "What we need to know is if you saw or heard anything last night."

I thought about the face at the window, the face that didn't look like mine, but for the sake of my sanity, I had to believe it was my own reflection, even though, deep down, I didn't "I don't believe this. You have two police at the top of the lane, two patrolling up and down all night, allegedly, yet you're asking me if I know what went on here?"

Detective Simpson visibly bristled. "Our officers can't be everywhere at once."

"It's a small lane! And there's four of them!" I stood up and held up the palm of my hand to them. "Enough is enough. Every time something happens, you keep asking me what I know, and every single time I tell you I know nothing. And now there's four police here constantly, yet you're still asking me. If it's the woods that are the problem, why aren't they standing outside there instead of walking up and down, then they'll know if anyone goes in there, and they'll hear anything that happens in there."

I don't know why (maybe it was the face at the window which still scared me) but I suddenly felt sick and tired of being questioned all the time. "Don't you think that if I knew anything I'd tell you? I know all these people. I know the boys and their families. If I could help them in any way, I would. You wouldn't have to ask me if I know anything. I'd come looking for you to tell you first."

"Harold, we're just..."

"Enough!" I cut him off abruptly. "You wake me up early and ask me if I know anything. You could have asked me that as soon as you knocked at the door. I'd have told you no and it would have saved all this time. I know it's your job to ask questions, but this is my home. It's my life, and this whole questioning us all the time is so intrusive. It's so invasive. And it helps no one."

As I was talking, police vans with dogs arrived, along with the forensic van (which I recognised because it was all too familiar now) and other official looking people. "You don't even know what's happened to the boys yet or if they're actually in the woods, so even if I had heard or seen something, what difference would it make now? Clearly, you're all set to search the woods anyway, so do it."

I got up and went inside, taking my coffee cup and closing the screen door behind me. As they stood up to leave, I heard Detective Norman say, "Boy he's cranky when you wake him up, isn't he?" I laughed. Let them think that and it might stop them from waking me up again.

I put on the TV and made breakfast while I watched the news. I was on my second cup of coffee when a breaking news item came on about the bodies of three teenage boys being found in the woods in Mackarb.

Oh crap. Now the shit would hit the fan all over again. People were already scared and angry. Now three boys were dead at once. It hadn't taken long to find them, so they couldn't have been that far into the woods. I wondered how someone could kill all three at the same time. Were there three killers? Or did the kids go in there one at a time and confront just one killer? But that just didn't make sense. In fact, none of it made sense to me.

I carried on watching while I did the dishes. They replayed the interview of the four of us at the pub which made it look like we were reacting to what had just happened. Maybe it was their way of trying to stop even more people coming here.

There was a knock at the door. It was Isabel. "Can you believe what's happened?" she said. I led her into the kitchen, switched the kettle on and made two cups of coffee as we talked. She said, "Three boys. Do you know what happened to them?"

"Only what I saw on the news this morning."

"The police woke me up earlier banging on the door and asking if I heard or saw anything last night, and the boys were only missing then," she said.

"You mean they've only just found them now? But it was just on the news. How did the media know already?"

"I reckon it's because they live here now."

"True, they do. But still, it seems awfully fast. No doubt it won't be long until we hear the grisly details of what happened to the last of The Octo Gang. Speaking of which, let's go sit outside. No doubt our favourite detectives will be back to quiz us soon and fill us in on what happened. I actually yelled at them earlier."

"Really? Do tell," said Isabel, smiling in anticipation. We each picked up a cup of coffee and took it outside and sat on the sofa swing.

I told her how annoyed I was that they woke me up and said that they needed to talk to me so I had to get dressed and come outside and all they wanted was to ask me if I saw or heard anything the night before, which is something they could have asked me straight away because the answer was no, as always.

Isabel agreed with me. "I don't blame you. If they were searching the woods anyway, nothing you said could have helped right then."

"I know. I just thought, 'find the damn boys instead of wasting your time and mine on something that doesn't matter anyway.' And at that time, they didn't even know if the boys had gone into the woods or not."

"I agree. To be honest, it feels like they still think we have something to do with it all. Do they think we all have secret basement passageways into the woods and that's how we're sneaking kids in there to kill them?"

I laughed. "That's actually a good idea. I hadn't thought of anything like that. It would explain why no one sees them go into the woods."

"Ah, but how do they get to our secret basements in the first place?" she asked.

"A secret passage from somewhere in town? Who knows? I think the police just have no clue, so they start making things up. But I love the secret passages idea."

"Or maybe," she continued, "it's not us at all. It's that old house across the road that has a basement passageway and there's a crazy old guy living there, luring kids in."

I felt guilty all over again for knowing about Marvin but not telling anyone, and for not talking about him now. "You have a creative, yet somewhat disturbing, mind. Just don't tell the media about your secret passageway idea or they'll be over there digging up the back yard looking for it."

"Speaking of the media," she said, "my ex-husband got in touch with me online. He saw me being interviewed on TV and the reporter saying I live in Forrest Lane. So, he asked me how things are going here. For years I haven't heard from him and he had no idea where I lived, but he does now."

"What did he want?"

"Nothing. I think he just wanted me to know that he knows where I am."

"What did you do?"

"He said, 'I know where you are now, Izzy.' Ugh! I blocked him."

"Izzy?"

"Yeah, he used to call me that all the time. I hated it."

"Poor Izzy."

"Don't ever call me that," she said, in the way that women often do when they sound like they're half joking, but you know they're seething and if you say it again, they'll kill you. "Got it," I said, raising my hands in surrender.

"So, who are the three boys?" she asked.

"Let me see. It must be Bishop Green, Noah French, and AJ Bronson."

"What does AJ stand for?"

"No idea. Everyone has always called him AJ and I was never interested enough to ask."

She smiled in understanding (we really were on the same wavelength on a lot of things) and said, "Do you know what I'm NOT going to do today, or for the next few days?"

"What?"

"Go into town. Can you imagine the mood of the place? I don't think I could handle it."

"How about we go out of town for lunch. Go somewhere no one knows us. We'll drive for an hour and see where we end up."

Isabel smiled and looked like she really liked that idea. "That sounds like the best thing I've heard in a long time. But there's only one problem."

"What's that?"

"Do we have to come back?"

I knew exactly how she felt. Being around the locals didn't feel good anymore and if you dared smile or look like you were enjoying yourself, you were vilified. No one smiled any more. No one dare.

"Pack a bag for a few nights. It's going to be a long lunch. At least a 3-day lunch I think."

Isabel smiled and instantly relaxed. "When are we going?"

"As soon as we finish our coffee." Just as I said that the gate opened. It was the two detectives.

"Back so soon? What is it now?" I asked them.

Detective Simpson spoke first. "We really need to talk to you." They both nodded in greeting to Isabel.

We all sat down together at the table. Detective Simpson said, "I know I've asked you before, but now I need to ask you again, both of you. Did you hear or see anything at all last night. ANYTHING."

He seemed desperate for an answer. I said, "Why? What's happened?" I was facing the street and I could see people rushing around, taking apparatus out of the vehicles and into the woods. More and more crime scene investigators were arriving too.

He took a deep breath and said, "It's the boys. The way they were found you must have heard something or seen something. Did you see anyone at all going into the woods?"

I again had that sudden flash of guilt about not mentioning Marvin. "My answer hasn't changed no matter what you found. What is that makes you so sure we must have seen or heard something?"

"What we found is disturbing. We've already sent officers to talk to the boys' parents. We're hoping they might know something, but it's doubtful. Our only hope right now is that those nearest the woods heard or saw something. Did you hear anything at all?"

"Like what? I'm not sure what you think we might have heard."

Detective Simpson leaned forward as though he was about to impart a secret. "It's the way the boys were found."

"Yeah, you said that."

"People's memory fades and gets distorted quickly about what they see and hear, so if there is anything, I want you to tell me now, no matter how insignificant you think it is.

I thought about the face at the window, but even if I told them, which I wasn't going to, it wouldn't be of any help to them. So, I simply said, "Tell us what's happened."

He took another deep breath and looked uncomfortable about what he was about to say, and once I heard it, I wasn't surprised. "We found all three boys laying together. All dead. Every part of them." A pause and another deep breath. "I say every part, because their bodies weren't complete. They all had two arms and two legs, but it wasn't their own arms and legs. They'd been swapped around."

There was a long silence while Isabel and I tried to digest what he'd just said. Neither of us knew what to say, so we said nothing.

Detective Simpson carried on. "Each boy had one arm from each of the other two and one leg from each of the other two, and they were laid out as though, um, they were doing, um... jumping jacks."

The picture he'd painted in my mind made me queasy. The look on Isabel's face was one of sadness mixed with horror. The whole thing was so disturbing, and I didn't know what to say.

Detective Simpson spoke first. "This is why I wanted to come and ask you as soon as I could. Did you hear anything at all. Screaming? Talking? Any movement in the woods? Whatever it is, no matter how small, it could be vital."

Isabel and I were silent. She was staring into the woods, while I looked at the veranda floor. Eventually I said, "How the hell is this all happening? It just doesn't make sense. I know these boys have been trouble, but to do this to them?"

"I know," said the usually silent Detective Norman. "We have the same issue with it all. I mean, who the hell would want these boys dead? Not only dead but want to do all this to them, from scaring them to death to ripping them apart?"

There really was nothing more to say, so we stayed silent. After a while Detective Simpson said, "Okay, we'll leave it for now but if you remember any tiny detail about last night, let me know straight away." I nodded.

When they'd gone, Isabel and I sat in silence for a while, idly watching all the people rushing in and out of the woods. Then she went home, and we both packed and got out of there, even though it was difficult to get my car out of the crowded and busy lane. We drove in total silence until we were far away from Mackarb. An hour later we pulled into a motel, booked a room with a kitchenette for three nights, went out for groceries and drinks and stayed in the room till we left three days later.

At first it felt somewhat selfish to drive away and leave all the problems of Mackarb behind. But after an hour or two, it was a relief. We had lunch that first day with a couple of beers that we drank at the little bistro table outside our room on the walkway, and then went back inside for an intimate afternoon.

By the next morning, we felt completely at ease and were happy to be away. Even if we'd stayed in Mackarb, there was nothing we could have done to help. It felt great to be able to sit around and do nothing. We ate, drank coffee, drank alcohol, talked, watched TV (but not the news), talked more, laughed a lot, and enjoyed being together on our own. It was a break we both needed, and I can easily say it was the best and most relaxing holiday I've ever had.

The only downside was that we had to leave. When we got home, even though the mood everywhere was mournful, I felt less tense after having a break from it all, especially a break with Isabel. I put on the news to catch up on what had happened since we'd been away. But it seemed nothing had happened, and the police still had no clue what was going on.

For the next few days, nothing more happened, and the lane cleared of non-residents, except for the usual police at the top of the lane in front of the barrier, and the two patrolling officers, not that their presence had stopped the murders. In fact, they'd increased them, with three boys dying at once this time.

But those three were the last of the gang of eight teens so I wondered if the killings would stop now. Hopefully it was over but either way, the woods would never feel like a safe place again. And every single person in Mackarb, would probably never recover.

But I'd seen Marvin go into the woods late in the afternoon on the same day the boys went missing.

I needed to speak to him and find out what he was really up to. There were too many coincidences. It was time to get to the truth.

# Going, Going, Gone

Somehow, since we returned home from our brief vacation, Isabel and I agreed that it would be best to spend our time together further away from the woods, so we started meeting up at her house at the top of the lane. The only major inconvenience was that the police were still stationed there in front of the barrier, 24/7, so they saw me going in and out of her house and knew how long I stayed.

On Saturday, I'd gone round there for lunch, and we'd spent the whole afternoon together. At dusk I walked back home. As I got near my place, I saw Marvin coming out from the side of his house. He turned as though he was heading into the woods. I called to him. He turned to look at me but made no move, so I walked over to him.

I looked up the lane as I went, hoping that the patrolling police would see Marvin too, but they were stood at the top, their backs turned towards us, chatting with the police at the other side of the barrier. I wished I was one of those people who could curl my thumb and index finger into my mouth and do a loud whistle to get their attention, but I couldn't whistle at all, so once again it looked like I was going to be the only person to see Marvin.

I wasn't sure what I was going to say to him. Conversations in my head always seemed straight forward, but when it actually came to talking face to face with someone, it seemed much more awkward. "Hey Marvin."

"Harold," he said with a slight nod.

"So, you know what happened to those three boys in the woods?" I asked him.

"Yes," he said in his usual straight forward way.

"I saw you going into the woods not long before those boys went missing."

"Yes." His answers, though short and to the point, always made it hard to know what to say next.

"I've seen you around several times when things have happened to the teenagers, so I have to ask you, did you have anything to do with any of it?" I felt like a fool for asking but I didn't know what else to say.

Marvin didn't react physically at all. He didn't tense up or change his expression. He simply answered in his usual monotone, cryptic way. "Harold, sometimes a lesser tragedy has to happen to stop an even bigger tragedy happening in the future."

That didn't answer my question, but he was good at doing that. "Well, did you?"

"The teenagers previous destructive attitudes and actions were always headed to a collision with a huge catastrophe."

"You're not making sense!" His vague answers annoyed me.

Without missing a beat or showing any emotion, he said, "The teenagers needed to be stopped. Sometimes nature takes its revenge."

"The woods? Are you saying the woods killed them?"

"Must be. What other explanation could there be?"

I tried to think of a logical answer, but nothing came to mind. Marvin doing the killing was the only explanation I had. He was a weird guy (or alien?), capable of doing weird things. Why else would he live in a house in the dark and manage to avoid being seen by everyone? I never even saw him come home with groceries or saw him in town. And how, on such a small street, did the other neighbours never see him? He must have to walk past their houses to get anywhere. And even the police hadn't seen him, and they were here permanently.

Marvin said, "Some call it Kama." He paused and looked at the woods then turned to me, and staring me straight in the eyes, in the unsettling way that he usually did, he said, "As I told you, I came here to work, but now my work is finished and so I'm going home. Goodbye Harold."

Without even waiting for me to respond, he turned and walked into the woods. Even though it was getting dark, I could see him as he walked through the trees until he eventually vanished into the darkness.

I stood there staring for a few minutes. Was he coming back? Did he mean that he was going home through the woods? Or was he going into the woods before he went home? He didn't have any luggage with him so he must be coming back. But where was he going? The police had blocked off entrances to the woods so he couldn't go anywhere. Or could he? Marvin was certainly an enigma. But I somehow had the feeling that I was never going to see him again.

I didn't want to leave the mystery of Marvin there. I wanted to know who (or what) he was. I made the bold decision to search his house for clues. I briefly scanned the street to see if anyone was looking. The police were still busy chatting and no one else was around. I slipped down the side of Marvin's house and went around to the back door. It was an old, thick, wooden door with a round doorknob and a large keyhole for a large old fashioned style key.

I tried the doorknob. It turned easily and the door opened. I let go, scared that a hand would shoot out from the darkness inside and grab my wrist, but nothing happened. The door creaked open slowly, the noise adding to my fear. If this was a movie I was watching on TV I'd be thinking 'Don't go in there,' knowing that something bad was going to happen.

But this wasn't a movie, this was real life, so it wasn't inevitable that something bad would happen, or at least I tried to convince myself. I briefly thought that maybe I should wait till morning to do this instead of creeping around when it was almost dark. But I was already here, and I knew that if I turned around now, I'd never come back. And I wanted to see if he'd left anything behind that would give me a clue about him.

I took a deep breath to mentally brace myself, then put my hand on the middle of the door and pushed it wide open. Inside was a small laundry room. On the opposite wall there was an old laundry sink on one side and an electric socket and space for a washing machine on the other side. There was an open doorway in the middle.

I was shaking but determined to do this. I felt along the wall just inside the back door and found the light switch. Click! The room was instantly bathed in a strange yellow light from the small, bare light bulb hanging on a wire from the ceiling. The room beyond was dimly lit through the doorway. I nervously stepped inside, pushing the door wide against the wall so that it was fully open and less likely to slam shut on me. I took another step. The laundry room was so small that in the one step I was standing just outside the opposite doorway.

I turned and looked behind me. The backyard looked completely black from in here. I was at a crossroads. I could go into the dark in front of me or the dark behind me. I stood, breathing heavily, ears alert for the faintest sound, but there was nothing but an unnerving silence.

I leaned forward trying to see further into the room beyond. It was an old kitchen. I could see a sink and countertop opposite, with cabinets above and below it, all along the wall. I wanted to go in, but my body seemed reluctant to move. I was afraid of who or what might be hiding at either side of the doorway, in the dark.

Then I thought of what would happen if I was wrong and Marvin hadn't left for good. What if I turned round and saw him standing at the back door?

Just the thought of that happening made my mind up. Being there with Marvin would be way scarier than being there alone. I turned and walked out into the darkness of the back yard. Fear affected the way I moved and even though it was only two steps, I stumbled along like I was drunk. As I went, I flicked the light switch off with one hand, grabbed the doorknob with the other, and slammed the door shut behind me, making sure that if anyone was in there, they couldn't follow me out.

And I didn't stop there. I kept half-walking half-stumbling around to the side of the house where it was slightly less dark than the back yard. I leaned against the house in relief, feeling like I'd just escaped something terrible. I looked across the road at my house, longing to be there in the safety of my own home.

I walked as far as the front yard of Marvin's house and stopped. I wanted to go home, but I also wanted to know about Marvin, and I knew that if I left now, that would be it. I'd never know. I knew it was stupid to go back in there when I'd only just gotten out, especially after I'd been so scared, but I just had to do it. I had to know.

This time, I'd be fast. I'd go straight in, putting lights on as I went, have a quick look around, then out. I reckoned I could be in and out in less than two minutes. It sounded like a good plan. Don't think about it, just do it. I took a few deep breaths to ready myself.

When I felt confident enough, or as confident as I could, I turned and set off back round the house before I could change my mind. I went straight to the back door, turned the knob and pushed. That's when I got an even bigger fright. The door wouldn't open. I tried again and again, but it wouldn't budge. It was locked. I bent down and looked at the gap between the door and the frame. Being an old door it was a wide gap. With the help of the bright moonlight, I could see the bolt was shut. That bolt could only be closed with a key. Yet it was closed.

I stood up straight. How could the door be locked, I'd just been in there? I bent down and looked again. The bolt was definitely closed. I took a step back and stared at the door. Did someone lock it after I left? My heart hammered in my chest. Did they lock it from the outside or the inside? Had the key been in the inside of the lock? If it had I wouldn't have seen it because I'd pushed the door as wide as it would go against the wall as I stepped inside. Had it been in the lock the whole time? It didn't matter.

I ran.

I ran around the corner of the house, down the side, out the front, across the road, and into my own front yard. Only once behind the safety of my own gate did I stop and look back at Marvin's house. It sat in darkness as usual.

"Are you okay, Harold?"

The voice made me jump. I hadn't seen the two policemen in the lane. They must have been walking down as I ran (bolted?) across the road. It wasn't until I tried to speak that I realised I was panting. "Yeah, yeah, I'm fine."

"What were you doing over there? Did you see something?" They both looked over at Marvin's house and then back at me.

"No, didn't see a thing."

"Why were you running?"

I suddenly felt stupid. How could I tell them the truth, that the door was open and then it was locked, and it scared me. "Boogey man," was all I could think to say.

"You saw the Boogey man?" They exchanged a questioning glance.

"No. I was just worried I might. I was having a nosey around when it suddenly occurred to me that this is not a good time to be wandering around alone in the dark."

"Did you go inside?"

I relaxed slightly because I could answer that one honestly. "No. It's locked." I didn't want them to ask me any more questions, so I ended the conversation quickly. "Well, goodnight." I turned and walked away, before they had a chance to say anything else.

I went inside, showered and made myself some dinner. All the while I thought about Marvin and how no one had known he was there. Even his next-door neighbours had never seen him in the back yard. Janet and Trevor who lived in the house next to Marvin had always referred to it as 'the empty house next door.'

Questions about Marvin kept going round and round in my head. He'd always been cryptic with everything he said and never seemed to give a straight answer to anything. Was that because he had something to hide or was it because he didn't actually know anything?

The mystery about Marvin would have to remain a mystery. Or maybe I just had to be patient and wait till other things were revealed in the future that might give me a clue as to whether or not it was Marvin who had committed all those murders.

And if it wasn't Marvin, then who?

# The Burning

For a while, I thought that the nightmare was over. All eight of The Octo Gang were dead, and as tragic as that was, the local consensus was that the killings would now stop, which seemed to lift the mood a little, in a strange, morbid way.

Our small town had suffered, there was no denying that, but feeling like it was over, was like waking up from a bad dream, except for the families whose sons had been murdered.

The police still had no clue as to who had killed all those young boys, and either did anyone else. It wasn't just that they were murdered, but the horrendous way it was done. Who would want to do that? Who had a mind sick enough to do that?

I was sitting on my front veranda in the evening, looking at the entrance to the woods, and pondering the whole situation when I suddenly got the heebie jeebies. One minute I was sitting and having a good old think about everything, when suddenly I felt vulnerable sitting outside in the dark and wanted to run inside. I didn't exactly run, but I did move indoors swiftly.

I locked the front door behind me and went to check the back door too. It was locked, which was a relief because how I felt right now, if it had been unlocked, I would have had to go around the whole house making sure no one had snuck in. I used to feel so safe in my own home, but not anymore.

Maybe someday I'd feel safe again, but not yet. The face at my window that night and Marvin's door being unlocked and then locked had scared the heck out of me. It was over two weeks since Marvin disappeared into the woods, and I'd tried to look around his house once he'd gone. Two whole weeks and it still unsettled me just looking at his dark, empty house across the road.

Over the next couple of months, the police presence lessened in our street and the two patrolling officers walking up and down ceased. It was a relief to us all in one way, but it left us feeling a bit vulnerable in another way, even though their constant presence hadn't stopped the kids being killed.

We'd all been interviewed by the police a couple more times just to make sure we hadn't seen anything or heard anything. The police really were desperate for any information, no matter how small or insignificant it might seem.

My favourite reporter, Susan Jackson, stopped me a few times asking for an interview. I told her that I didn't have anything new to tell her, but she still wanted tidbits about how sad or scared everyone was feeling, but I couldn't tell her much about that either, yet I still saw myself on the news constantly, the same interviews being played over and over again. I guess when there's no news they keep replaying the old stuff.

One thing that I did know about how everyone was feeling, was that they all wished the media would leave them all alone. They were sick of our town being shown on TV and they all resented the media intrusion. But I couldn't tell Susan that, even though it was now the most talked about subject.

With nothing much happening here now, the media people started moving out of the hotel. I was surprised that they stayed so long given that the hotel accommodation was a few rooms upstairs all opening onto a narrow wooden veranda with a shared bathroom at each end. Not exactly luxury accommodation, but it's the only accommodation we have in town, except for a small caravan park that can only host about 20 caravans before it's full, and it's usually full of locals living there in their vans.

Susan was the last of the media people to leave, staying a full week longer than the others. After she went it was a much more pleasant experience walking into town without a microphone being shoved in my face and a TV camera lighting me up. I was never sure why those cameras needed to glare a light in our faces even when it was a bright sunny day.

With the media people gone, I decided to go for lunch at the pub with Isabel. We met up with a few others while we were there and spent 3 hours together, talking, eating, drinking, and (sometimes) laughing when the subject got off the murders.

Afterwards, Isabel and I took a leisurely stroll back to Forrest Lane, holding hands the whole time. We spent the rest of the afternoon intimately at her house, and then had dinner.

At ten o'clock I left to go home. Isabel asked me to stay, but I'm always happier waking up in my own bed in my own home, and we'd already been together for over 10 hours, and I wanted to relax on my own for a while.

I got a beer from my fridge, twisted off the top, and took it outside to the front veranda. I sat on the sofa swing and for the first time in weeks, I felt comfortable being outside at night. The two police officers were still guarding the barrier at the top of the lane, but no one was down this end, and it was peaceful now that my heebie jeebies had gone.

I sat in silence, the only noises coming from the woods, the usual sounds of nature. I took a few swallows of my beer and enjoyed my quiet time alone.

I must have only sat there for about 10 minutes when a noise startled me. It was only a soft noise. It was the sound of someone walking on grass, which was brown and crunchy with all the dry weather we'd been having, and it sounded like it was coming up the side of my house. My head snapped to the side to look in the direction the footsteps were coming from. Then the noise stopped. I stared at the corner of the house, terrified about what might be there, just out of sight.

My spine was so tense it hurt. I was breathing hard but trying to do it quietly so that I wouldn't miss a sound, thinking the whole time about what I'd do if the sound started again, and that my only 'weapon' was the glass bottle in my hand.

I wanted to get up and flee to the safety of indoors, but I daren't turn my back on whoever or whatever might be there. When I didn't hear any more, I began to doubt myself. Did I really hear something? Could it just have been a small rodent? Or was it the face of whoever was there before, looking at me through the window. My heart thumped so hard in my chest I could feel it against my ribs. The waiting was agonising. I must have waited only a few seconds, but it felt much longer.

Suddenly the soft walking sound came again, and then a dark figure appeared from around the corner of the house.

I stood up and made a terrified noise that sounded like "Errrrrr!" My heart pounded even harder than before. My hand shook so hard that beer slopped over my fingers that were clutching the bottle tightly, but my eyes were glued to the person standing in the dark, looking at me. I wanted to run but I daren't. I was mesmerised and wanted to know who was there. All I could make out was a silhouette, but I could tell it was a woman.

"Hello Harold," said the familiar voice of the reporter, Susan Jackson. "I wasn't sure if you'd be out here this late or not."

At that moment I wasn't sure if knowing it was her was less frightening or not. "What are you doing here?" I asked her, trying not to let my voice tremble.

"Ending it all," she said, matter of factly.

"Your life?" I wasn't sure what she meant.

"Everything. It all needs to end now."

"I thought it was ended."

"No. I've spent years waiting for my chance for revenge, and now there's nothing left for me."

"Susan, you're not making sense. Sit down." I indicated the table and chairs.

She came onto the veranda, pulled out a chair and sat facing me. I sat down opposite her.

She looked towards the entrance to the woods and said, "It all started in there and tonight it's going to end in there."

"The murders? Do you mean the murders happened in there?"

She looked me straight in the eye. "No, the suicide. My son committed suicide in there."

I suddenly knew what she was talking about. My shoulders slumped as the tension left them. "Oh God, Susan. That was your son? Terry. Was his name Terry?"

She half smiled at me. "You remembered his name, that's nice. No one else remembers who he was. He means nothing to them, and those boys were allowed to go on living, with no punishment for what they did."

"I'll never forget his name. It was a long time ago, and I thought it was so sad. It touched me for quite a while."

Susan continued to stare at the entrance to the woods, her face sad, her words emotionless. "I remember when I came here after he died, you were the only person who spoke to me. I was standing down there, looking into the woods, when you walked up to me, and you were very kind. I could tell you cared about what happened to Terry. No one else did. The parents of those eight boys even accused me of trying to cause trouble for their sons. Can you believe that?" She choked out the last sentence with a sob.

My mind went back to her son dying. It must have been about seven or eight years ago. All the boys were in primary school. I remembered hearing about an eight-year-old who'd gone into the woods and killed himself. He'd taken a length of wire, wrapped it round and round a tree branch, made a noose in the end and hung himself. I'd seen on the news that a small stool had been found near him and that he must have used it to reach the branch to tie the wire, and to jump off when he'd finished.

It was also well known that he'd been bullied both physically and mentally at school by a group of eight boys. The teachers had been reluctant to do anything about it, telling the boy to simply "stay away" from the bullies. Even after his death, they refused to believe that the bullying had led to his suicide.

I did remember seeing the boy's mother at the entrance to the woods after it happened, and talking to her, but she was a chubby woman with short dark hair. Susan was slim and had long blonde hair. And the boy's name wasn't Jackson. I couldn't quite remember at that moment, but I was sure it wasn't Jackson.

"That was you that day? You look so different."

She smiled sadly. "I used to live in the next village, which is why Terry went to school in Mackarb, it's the only school around here. I was married then, and now I'm divorced, so I use my maiden name again. I couldn't get over what happened to my son. My husband divorced me after two years and moved on. I moved away to where no one knew me or knew what happened to my boy. I got a job, lost weight, and changed my hair colour. I changed everything about my life. I drank a lot, I cried a lot, and I had one-night stands with quite a few men, all those changes were nothing like the woman I used to be, but I didn't care anymore."

She looked at me and I could see the depth of the sadness in her eyes as the past flooded back to her as she spoke. "Then one day it hit me. The reason I felt so bad was because those boys and their parents had gotten away with what they did. But not anymore. I made up my mind to make them pay. My life was over when I lost Terry, and nothing seemed to matter anymore. But his life did matter.

"I decided right there and then that those parents were going to lose their sons, in the woods, where I lost my son. I didn't know how I was going to do it, but it didn't matter. I just knew that I would, and I'd sort out the details over time. That's when I became a freelance writer, and a TV channel hired me to write up their news stories for their presenters to read. It was interesting work and it paid well, plus I had time to do my other writing projects for other clients too. I was popular as a writer. Then I talked the TV company into hiring me as a reporter and they were happy to."

She looked towards the woods again. "I knew I could never come back here until my plan was ready to execute. I couldn't stand seeing this place, but I had to if I wanted to work my plan, and as the months and years went on, I worked on what I was going to do to those boys, and how I was going to do it. That's when I knew I had to come back here and find out where the boys lived and how I was going to coax them to go into the woods."

Susan looked back at me with a sorrowful smile and said, "And as I looked around here, in disguise, of course, I discovered that the boys had started hanging out in the woods all on their own. How serendipitous was that? So, I moved my plan forward and began it sooner than I'd anticipated, and the TV station let me be the reporter who covered the story. Do you see how useful that was?"

I didn't know what to say, so I just shook my head.

"You see, Harold, I was able to get myself into the investigation with the police, so I knew what they were doing and if they had any clues as to who was killing those boys. I also knew what sort of clues they were looking for because I had long discussions with the crime scene people and asked them what sort of evidence they were collecting. I pretended that it was for an in-depth program about these crimes that the TV network were thinking of doing once this whole thing was over. And they bought it and were happy to tell me anything I wanted to know. And what I really wanted to know was what evidence to NOT leave behind which helped me so much and made everything go much more smoothly."

Susan went silent, staring into the woods again with a look of resignation. I could see she was tired. She was no longer the bubbly reporter. Clearly that had been a facade, and a very good one. No one guessed that she had such dark, hidden, secrets.

"Susan, I have to ask you, and I don't want it to sound too morbid, but how did you do it? The police couldn't fathom the timelines or how you got in and out of the woods without being seen. And I couldn't either. I sit out here most nights and the police were marching up and down here for weeks."

Her gaze remained on the entrance to the woods. Her words were monotone as though she didn't care about what she'd done. "It was easy to scare that first kid. I used a few scary noises to lure him away from his friends and then a scary mask, which I guess looked even more terrifying out there in the dark. Scared him to death. Literally." She let out a small laugh.

"As to the kid up against the tree with an arrow through his heart. That was easy. I snuck up and stabbed him first and wheeled him away. Then I wheeled him back, sat him up against the tree, and let him have it with my bow and arrow. Archery is something I've been practicing, just for that moment, and I got pretty good at hitting a target, even one as small as a heart. Boom! Pinned him to the tree." She suddenly laughed, amused at her own callousness.

"The next kid, I broke his back good. It was just sheer luck that he crossed the road in front of me when I was driving back from a meeting at the TV studio. I was just coming into Mackarb when I saw the little bastard, so I put my foot down hard and WHAM!" She gave a small laugh. "That little sucker flew over my car and hit the road behind me. So, I gathered him up, threw him in my boot, and drove him to the woods to be found. His spine was so twisted his backside was at the frontside. It was awesome.

"And then there was the kid found with no eyes. I gotta say the birds were helpful with that one. I'd used the noises and the mask again on him, and then slugged him a good one in the face which broke his jaw, knocked him unconscious, and he bled out. Not very exciting but the pecked-out eyes added an unexpected, final touch."

She was silent again and looked as though she was reliving the events she'd spoken about. Then she turned to look at me. "I saw you Harold. I saw you searching for him. I'd covered him up until then, but I uncovered him just for you."

Her admission took me by surprise. I said, "I thought I wasn't the only one in there at the time. I had no idea it was you."

She gave a sad smile. "I saw you run away too." Then she looked back at the woods and said, "Do you want to know how I did the kid buried alive? How I dug that hole so quick?"

I was taken aback by the unexpected question. "I have to say I'm somewhat morbidly intrigued, but only because it seemed impossible at the time."

She shrugged slightly. "It was really quite easy. Forward planning and digging, and camouflage till needed. Getting him to come to me was easy too. Teenage boys are so gullible. It was also easy to drug him with something that wouldn't show in an autopsy, so that it looked like he'd been buried willingly, and also so that I could bury him quickly without him fighting. I didn't have much time, but I didn't need it.

"It was just as easy with the last three. That was well planned, easy to get them there as always, then all I needed was a sharp saw blade, and my own efficiency to get the job done."

I had one last question. "But how did you get in there? The police were all over the place stopping anyone from going into the woods."

She looked me in the eye and said, "Clearly, they didn't stop everyone. I got in and out without being seen, just like the kids. I'd already searched for a way in before I started it all. It's impossible to block every single entry. Those woods are huge. But now my job is done. The boys are dead, and their parents will never get over what happened to them. That's been the best part of it all, watching them suffer."

"You know, the police might catch you."

She laughed and said matter-of-factly, "No. They won't." Then she looked at me seriously and said, "There's just one more part of my plan. The finale. Just when everyone thinks it's over, this will make them scared all over again."

I had a horrible feeling that I knew what she was going to do. "You're going into the woods, aren't you."

She looked away and said, "Yes, Harold. I'm going to join my son. We've been apart too long." Without saying another word, she stood up and walked away.

I watched her go into the woods. She walked slowly and with purpose. I thought about calling the police or running and trying to stop her, but what was the point? How she ended her life was her choice. She'd planned it all along. No doubt whatever she was going to use to do it, was already in there waiting for her right where she'd left it.

I sat and stared at the woods, waiting to see or hear whatever was going to happen. For a while there was no noise at all. Then deep in the woods something flared bright yellow/orange. Fire. It appeared so fast she must have used an accelerant. The fire intensified instantly, and I couldn't yet be certain, but I was sure I heard her scream, "Terry!" Within seconds I could smell the fire as well as see it.

I went inside to get my phone and called emergency services to tell them there was a fire in the woods.

Then I calmly went back outside, with another beer, to watch the commotion that was about to engulf our small lane once again.

# Meanwhile, Back at The Campfire...

"Wow!" exclaimed Roger, sitting back in his camp chair. "So, it was the reporter all along."

"What was the fire?" asked Douglas. "Is that how she killed herself?"

"Yep," I said. "Unsurprisingly she not only set herself on fire, but also the tree her son had hung himself from. It took a few days for the police to figure out who's the burnt body was."

"Didn't you tell them?" asked Roger.

"No. I pretended I knew nothing about it. I didn't want to get involved in any of it or spend hours explaining it to the police, who probably would've suspected that I had something to do with it."

"What about the locals in Mackarb? How long did they go on thinking that the killer had struck again?" asked Douglas.

"To this very day. The panic that the killer had struck again went on for weeks if not months. I tried to stay away from everyone because it was hard to listen to them all speculating and worrying, and I was dying to tell them. The only person I did tell was Isabel."

"Aren't you worried that she'll tell others?" asked Roger.

"No. I trust Isabel 100%. Besides, I knew she wouldn't want the hassle of dealing with the police if we told them the truth. The kids were all dead and so was the killer. We knew nothing else was going to happen, so we just waited it out until it all calmed down. Now it's just an unsolved murder."

"So, the three of us and Isabel are the only ones who know the truth?" asked Douglas.

"I guess so."

"But aren't you dying to tell everyone what really happened?"

"Not at all. If there was a conclusion to this story it would be made into a movie and be on all the crime shows. As it stands, it's an unsatisfactory story because there is no ending. Just idle speculation."

"What about Marvin?" asked Roger. "Did you find out more about him? Did he have anything to do with it all?"

"Well, that's the most interesting thing about it all, and once I knew who he was, it all started to make sense."

"Oh my God!" said Roger. "This just keeps getting better. Who was he?"

"Well, I had no idea until Susan mentioned him." I said. "Just before she went into the woods for the final time, I said to her that I couldn't believe that she'd done all this on her own, and that's when she told me. She said that she'd had some help from her father, Marvin, who'd been devastated about what had happened to his grandson. And that's when it all made sense. He was hiding in the house so no one knew he was there so that he could help her."

"But why was there never any lights on?" asked Douglas.

"Because he wasn't living there. He was only there when Susan needed him, which is why I only ever saw him when a murder was about to happen or when one had just been committed. It also explained why he was so cryptic and didn't want to talk much, because he didn't want to give too much away. It also explained his reasoning that the murders were nature taking revenge. With hindsight I don't think he said nature."

"What did he say?" asked Roger.

"I think he said nurture. In their minds, the last thing Terry's mother and Grandfather could do for him, was punish The Octo Gang for what they did to him.

"But why did no one else see Marvin?" asked Douglas.

"He wasn't seen because he was careful not to be seen. Whenever I saw him going into the woods, he was probably going home or going to meet up with Susan. Using the woods also meant that he never needed to walk up the lane either."

"That still doesn't explain why the back door to the house was locked when you went back that night," said Roger.

"Yeah," I said. "I thought about that one too and the only answer is that Marvin wasn't leaving when he said he was, he was just making an excuse as to why he was going into the woods. So, when I went to the back door he watched me then came back and hid in the back yard and locked the door as soon as I left, not knowing that I was going to come straight back. But he probably didn't care anyway because it just added to the mystery of him."

"What happened to his house?" asked Roger. "Is it still empty?"

"Oh no. Once the lane was opened back up to the public, that place was snapped up. Like I said, the relatives who owned it were arguing about it for years, but I heard that the offer they got was so high, none of them wanted to turn it down.

"The weird thing is though, the family who bought it, renovated it somewhat before they moved in. But they only stayed a few months and then sold it, and then it was sold again a few months later, and then again. There must be something weird about that house because it seems no one wants to live there for long."

"Do you think that's because of Marvin?" asked Douglas.

"How can it be?" I asked.

"You know, like he's left some sort of aura behind him, or bad vibes, or something like that. You hear about houses where something bad happened and then no one wants to live there."

"Nothing bad happened there. At least I don't think so."

"Never mind that," said Roger, looking at me and smiling "let's get onto the important stuff now. What happened between you and Isabel? Does that story have a happy ending?"

I smiled at them both. "You betcha. Isabel and I are getting married in a few weeks and you're both invited to the wedding."

"Is it in Mackarb?" asked Douglas. "That will be so cool if we can come there."

"Not only is it in Mackarb, it's in Forrest Lane, right next to the woods. We're getting married in my back yard. It's big enough to hold a large marquee and a lot of the locals are coming. It's one of the most talked about events in town right now."

"I can't wait," said Roger. "Not only do we get to meet Isabel and all your friends, we get to visit Mackarb. We can arrive a few days before and have a good look around and see where it all happened."

"It's going to be great," said Douglas. "Can we go into the woods?"

"Sure," I said, "but there's no guarantee you'll come out alive."

END